BROOKLYN
LOOPER

SEAN
FARLEY

Bloomington, IN   authorHOUSE®   Milton Keynes, UK

AuthorHouse™
1663 Liberty Drive, Suite 200
Bloomington, IN 47403
www.authorhouse.com
Phone: 1-800-839-8640

AuthorHouse™ *UK Ltd.*
500 Avebury Boulevard
Central Milton Keynes, MK9 2BE
www.authorhouse.co.uk
Phone: 08001974150

This book is a work of fiction. People, places, events, and situations are the product of the author's imagination. Any resemblance to actual persons, living or dead, or historical events, is purely coincidental.

First published by AuthorHouse 1/11/2007

ISBN: 978-1-4259-8116-7 (sc)
ISBN: 978-1-4259-8115-0 (hc)

Library of Congress Control Number: 2006910493

Printed in the United States of America
Bloomington, Indiana

This book is printed on acid-free paper.

Dedication

- - -

This book is dedicated to Erica Mongello, Jennifer Farley, and to my parents Richard and Lauri Farley.

Thank you for all of your help and your incredible support. I love you all.

PREFACE

As you read this book you may be able to tell that this is my first novel. In fact, with the exception of this one, I can count on one hand the number of books that I have read in my life. Unless of course, you count *Stuart Little*. That one I read once in 1979, but I did my book report on it every year from the fourth through the eighth grade. While most of the smarter kids were playing board games like *Dungeons and Dragons* and reading *The Hobbit,* I was running around the Roosevelt Field Shopping Mall on Long Island trying to find Cliffs Notes for the books that were on my grade-school mandatory reading list. I would do anything to avoid having to read. One time I even paid a kid twenty bucks for a bootleg version of *Huckleberry Finn* that his old man copied from his Sony Betamax onto a VCR tape so I could cut down on my Cliffs Notes reading.

People have told me that I tell a pretty good story. The "You should write a book" comment was something I never really took seriously until one day I thought, "What the hell, I'll give it a shot." Over the years, I've worked as a caddy, a bartender, a disc jockey, a deli clerk, a high school teacher, and for the past several years, a stockbroker. I have taken my real life experiences and combined them with two fictional characters, creating a book that will remind you of that unforgettable friend, who no matter what, never lets you down.

Brooklyn Looper is about one thing ... Friendship. Frankie Morelli and Eddie Mullaney, two high school kids from Brooklyn, give real meaning to that word, and they encounter a situation that will change their lives forever.

BROOKLYN LOOPER

Vinny Morelli was zipping his cab down Thirty-fourth Street at about fifty-five miles an hour on a cold afternoon in 1980. He had his off-duty sign lit up. He wasn't really off duty, officially, but he had to do something to lessen the amount of people who jumped off the curb, waving their hands in the air for a cab, considering nobody has any fuckin' idea when a cabbie is on or off duty in the Big Apple. Vinny had long, brown hair in the back of his head and a huge forehead. The front of his hair was thinning slightly. He was an olive-skinned Sicilian with a short fuse and a lead foot. He had two dark blue tattoos. He had one on his left arm with the number seven, as a tribute to his favorite Yankee, Mickey Mantle. The one on his right arm was of the interlocking *NY*, the New York Yankee logo.

Vinny was in a real hurry on this particular evening, not because he was hustling to pick up a fare, or in a hurry to get to Penn Station to take a piss, but because he just got word from another cabbie that his wife, Maryanne, was in labor at Victory Memorial Hospital in Brooklyn. Maryanne had phoned the cabstand, and begged the dispatcher to track Vinny down.

Vinny met Maryanne in 1977 when she was working as a waitress at a place called Jackie Margot's, a restaurant directly across the street from the cabstand. She was fifteen years younger than he was, and she was the hottest waitress in New York City. She was about five-two with a body that could stop a clock. She had thick brown hair, bright blue eyes, and she wore enough make-up to cover a fuckin' Carvel ice cream cake.

Vinny had worked in the Madison Square Garden area for thirteen years. He spent more time scalping tickets to Garden events than picking up fares with his cab. He was the poorest excuse for a ticket scalper in New York. He had been busted multiple times for scalping, yet he kept doing it. He didn't care, he was more than bold about it too. You see, most scalpers, when they're working their perspective sporting event, always use the phrase, "You sellin' tickets?" or "Yo, you sellin'?" Some even say "Excuse me sir, are you selling?" It all depends upon their target. These phrases are used by scalpers just to test the waters, to see if the target responds "No, but I'm *looking* for tickets." This way the scalper could always say that he didn't initiate the sale. The midtown cops were way too smart for that shit, and there was no way guys got away with it, even though they thought they could.

Vinny might as well have worn a sign on his back that read, "Scalper." He would walk around, wearing the jersey of whatever team was playing that night, be it Knicks, Rangers or St. John's. He even had a fuckin' Globetrotter jersey in his wardrobe. He would be at that Garden every night there was an event, yelling out loud "Yo, I got two," or "Best seats in the house right here." On or off cab duty, he didn't care. In fact, he enjoyed scalping while he was on cab duty. He felt like he was making double time. Any time a cop spotted him in action, he'd hop back into his cab and blend in with the rest of the cabs on the street. This was Vinny's life, but tonight was different.

"Mutha fucka!" he screamed, as he approached the light at the corner of Thirty-fourth Street and Seventh Avenue. He was forced to stop short because he wasn't paying attention. His wheels were screeching from braking too hard as he was looking through the passenger side window. He was completely distracted because he was watching his fellow scalpers doing their thing, as they got ready for the Knick game. Rodney, his main scalping competitor, smirked at Vinny and gave him the middle finger. Rodney was a tall black guy with a big afro. He looked exactly like Warren Coolidge, the hoops star, on the TV show "The White Shadow."

Vinny was banging his hands on the steering wheel, waiting for the red light to change. "I gotta get the hell out of this fuckin' city!" Rodney smirked again and Vinny began to yell in his direction out of his smoked filled window, "Fuck you, Rodney." He and Rodney were actually friends, but Vinny was easily agitated, and Rodney, along with everyone else within a three-mile radius of the Garden, knew it. They all loved to break his balls.

Vinny hung a quick right onto Seventh Avenue and then another quick right onto Thirty-first Street. All he could do was think about the Brooklyn Battery Tunnel. If he wasn't through that tunnel in the next ten minutes, he was screwed.

He had no idea how far into labor Maryanne was, and the thought of not being at the hospital for the birth of his first-born was killing him.

"Little Jeannie," by Elton John, was the popular song at this time, and it was cranking on his radio as he approached the Battery Tunnel. Vinny, although still upset that the tunnel was full of traffic, took a second to smile when he heard the song since Jean Marie was what he and Maryanne had decided they would name their kid if it was a girl. When the song ended, he was back to banging on that steering wheel and screaming at people. These people in front of him really had no control of their slow-moving vehicles, but he just stuck his head out of the window and yelled anyway. "Hurry up, goddamn it!"

There was nothing he could do. It was December 16th, right smack in the middle of the holiday season, in the busiest city in the world, and there was bumper-to-bumper traffic in the Brooklyn Battery Tunnel. He missed most of the Lamaze classes and really had no idea what the hell to do when he got there anyway. His relationship with his wife was mediocre at best, but he was just so excited to be having a kid. It took a while for them to have a baby and he was a rookie at the whole process. Like most guys the first time around, he was hoping for a boy, but a healthy baby was his main concern. Vinny was forty-seven years old. He had wintry lines in his face that looked as tattered as an old baseball glove from all of the cigarettes he had smoked over the years. He already smoked five or six in the tunnel. He was excited, scared and inexperienced, and he was flipping out more and more with each slow-moving mile.

I<small>T WAS</small> D<small>ECEMBER</small> 16, 1980 and trading on the New York Stock Exchange had just ended for the day, with the Dow Jones closing at 918.09. People were making a lot of money in 1980, even though the average daily trading volume was light, and the hustle and bustle of places like Penn Station and Grand Central Terminal was crazier than ever. Wally McDougal, a Wall Street floor broker, came stumbling out of the bathroom of Timothy Flynn's, a Penn Station bar, with a Long Island Railroad train schedule in his hand, bouncing into one wall after another. McDougal was about 195 pounds, with dark satin hair, a red booze-filled face, and blood shot eyes. He was about five-eight with five o'clock shadow on his face. He wore black-rimmed glasses that looked as if they had been stepped on a million times. He was wearing a black overcoat that was covered in dandruff, a white dress shirt with a loose green and white tie, and black dress pants.

McDougal was a real smart ass whose older brother had a ton of money and had set him up with a nice little job at his firm on the floor of the Stock Exchange. He was a hyperactive asshole with a lot of cash, a coke and alcohol problem, and a knack for pissing people off with his arrogance. As he was closing out his tab, he heard a train called over the loudspeaker. "Now boarding on Track 17, the 4:22 train to Port Washington making stops at Woodside, Flushing Main Street, Broadway, Auburndale, Bayside, Douglaston, Little Neck, Great Neck." McDougal yelled at the bartender, "Can ya hurry the fuck up, I'm gonna miss my fuckin' train."

The bartender was an old-timer with a hunchback and a full head of gray hair. He walked over towards McDougal, and despite the fact that he hated the way he was being spoken to, he was so excited to get rid of this asshole, that he simply smiled and handed him his receipt.

As McDougal made his way down the stairs to the train, he searched for the handrail immediately. The stock market had only closed a few minutes ago and by the look of him, you would think this guy had been out drinking all night. That's how bombed he was. He left work at 1:15 for lunch, and having an absentee boss for a brother, this shit just kind of went on quite often. Anyone who knows the rules on the floor of the New York Stock Exchange, knows that you eat where you stand. There are no lunch breaks.

McDougal staggered to the bottom of the stairs and frantically started slapping his hands on his legs and reaching in and out of his pockets. He screamed, "My wallet, my fuckin' wallet, somebody stole my fuckin' wallet." Not knowing what the hell to do, in part because of the crowd trying to get by him, but mostly because he was just too smashed to think straight, McDougal pushed his way back up the stairs into an oncoming stream of fast-moving people, looking for the first cop he could find. When he got to the top of the steps he realized that the last time he thought he had his wallet was when he got off the subway a few hours earlier, too drunk to realize that he just used it to pay his fuckin' bar tab. Determined to find his wallet, he by-passed the bar and headed right for the subway, swearing he had left it on the counter of a news stand by the No. 2 train. He headed up the platform weaving in and out of people. New York City subway platforms are typically very crowded. People were everywhere just waiting to get home. McDougal headed right for the news stand. He couldn't get through fast enough, so he decided to run between the yellow lines on the platform. This guy still thought he had a shot at catching the 4:22, and he was in a rush like it was life and death.

JOE MULLANEY SIGNED OUT FOR the day at his new office in lower Manhattan. He had been a New York City cop for five years, working in the 42nd Precinct in the Bronx. This was his first day working in Manhattan at his new job. He had been trying to get out of the Bronx for a while, and he really looked forward to this new challenge. He'd had a long day so far as he got used to his new surroundings, and to top it off, he got a flat tire on the West Side Highway in the car that had been assigned to him. He'd figured they gave all of the shitty cars to the new guys. He didn't care though. The day was over, and he was standing on the subway platform waiting to get home. He was beaming today, despite the fact that he still had to take the No. 2 train one stop to the No. 7 train. The No. 7 train smelled awful and had more graffiti on it than the ones shown in the fuckin' "Welcome Back Kotter" intro song. On any other day the sight of this train and the rancid smell on the platform would depress the shit out of him, but not today. Today was different. Just before he left work, he received a call from his wife, Kathy, that she had her first contractions. Their first-born was on the way and he couldn't wait to get home.

Joe was one of the burliest cops in all of the Bronx and his comrades hated to see him go. The mere sight of him would make guys surrender without a fight when he made a collar. He was about six-five with arms and legs like tree trunks. He was going bald and wore a buzz cut to hide his rapidly receding hairline. He had light eyebrows and a chubby nose. He was a tough looking Irish guy with a tattoo of Notre Dame's Fighting Irishman on his left arm.

Joe and his wife Kathy lived in a three-bedroom house in Woodside. He usually drove to work because he hated riding on trains, but since his wife was expecting, he wanted his car close to home. He left his blue 1975 Pontiac LeMans with his next-door neighbor, Pete Kerner. Pete was an electrician with Local 3. He was on a mandatory twelve-week furlough, so he was spending his time doing some side work. He was a little guy with brown hair that rose up about six inches off of his head.

Pete did body work on tons of cars in Woodside and Jackson Heights. This guy had a talent for fixing cars and he saved people a fortune. His prices were fair and he stayed in the garage all day until the job got done. Pete was an insane New York Jet fan. He would paint cars, wearing a real Ridell Jets helmet on his head, and when a customer would ask for a color suggestion, he would always suggest green and white. There were at least five Jet-mobiles on that Woodside street. All of them were the handy-work of Pete Kerner. He tried to coax Joe into going with green with white pin-striping on the LeMans, but Joe chose the Met colors instead. Pete and Joe caught a few Met games together every year, and would always meet for a cold one on Friday nights at the Garden Grill, the neighborhood pub down the street.

Joe was actually speaking aloud to himself as he was leaning against the wall waiting for his train. Nobody could hear him because the train was screeching into Penn Station. If you were there to read his lips as he leaned against that wall, you would see what he was saying. "Holy shit, I'm gonna be a dad tonight."

VINNY CAME WHIPPING INTO THE parking lot of Victory Memorial Hospital. He had already smoked a half a pack of non-filtered Camel cigarettes in traffic and he didn't give a shit where he parked his car. He slammed on the brakes with the ass of the car sticking out into the middle of the emergency room parking lot and left the car right under a huge sign that read NO PARKING ANYTIME. He got out of the car with a half-lit cigarette dangling out of his mouth and ran inside. He went up to the first desk he saw and yelled to the woman behind the desk, "Labor and Delivery please!" The gray haired woman behind the desk was sitting there chewing on a pencil and listening to a small transistor radio. Vinny had sweat running down his face and he was breathing heavily. The woman looked at him with a look of shock on her face and said, "Will you please put your cigarette out, sir?"

Vinny had smoke shooting out of his ears. "Are you fuckin' serious lady? I'm not a flower delivery guy here, my wife is having a baby."

"What's your wife's name?" asked the woman, frowning at Vinny, wanting so bad to curse right back at him, but resisting the temptation.

"Morelli, Maryanne Morelli!" Vinny was huffing and puffing like the Big Bad Wolf and he still had not put his cigarette out.

"Your wife is in labor, sir."

"How do I get there?"

She pointed with her right hand towards some swinging doors about twenty feet down the hall. "Right through those doors Mr. Morelli. Good luck sir, don't be so nervous and please, put your cigarette out. I don't think cigarette smoke is the first thing you want your child to smell."

Vinny smiled and apologized, extinguishing his cigarette in the sand-filled ashtray next to the pay phone. He ran away with his back towards the doors, still yelling to the woman at the desk, "Thank you so much, sorry I'm such a nut, thank you!"

Vinny ran through the doors, frantically, looking for anyone dressed in a white coat who could tell him where Maryanne was. Still breathing heavily, he grabbed a doctor. "Excuse me, Doc."

Before he could finish, the doctor said, "You must be Mr. Morelli."

"Yeah," said Vinny, with a look of confusion on his face as to how the hell this guy knew exactly who he was. "Where's my wife?"

"Right this way sir," said the doctor. "Hurry up, put this

gown and mask on."

As Vinny walked into the delivery room he could feel the beads of sweat running down his face and through his palms. Maryanne was propped up with her legs spread, breathing fast and sweating profusely. With the way her make-up was smeared all over her face, she looked like an angry raccoon. Maryanne's obstetrician, Dr. Sam Fischer, was encouraging her to push.

"Gimme a fuckin' epidural!" Maryanne was crying in pain and she was screaming all sorts of crazy things. "Knock me out, Dr. Fischer, please, knock me out, I can't take this, I can't, please. Do something, please!" She glanced out of the corner of her eye and there was Vinny. This wise-ass, smart-mouth, two-time loser, with the thickest skin in Brooklyn, was in complete shock at the pain this woman was enduring. Having cut most of the recently popular Lamaze classes, he didn't know what to do. Dr. Fischer began to tell Maryanne to breathe. He then looked over at Vinny and said, with an encouraging tone, "Come on Vinny, go stand right by Maryanne's head, come on, we need your help. It's okay, come on pal."

"Fuck him! If he didn't miss all of the goddamn classes he wouldn't be standin' there looking like he's gonna shit in his pants!" screamed Maryanne. Vinny's soft side was starting to show and he was actually crying at this point because he felt that bad for his wife.

"It's a boy!" yelled Dr. Fischer.

Maryanne was still gasping for air from this exhausting, yet beautiful experience. She was smiling and crying tears of joy, and so was Vinny. For two people who really didn't have the best marriage, this was a great experience, and to date, the most special day of their lives.

They were immediately two of the proudest people in Brooklyn, and they stared at each other in amazement, completely full of joy and elation.

Vinny spent most of the night on the payphone as Maryanne got some rest. He actually asked his cab customers all week long to pay with change if they had it, anticipating this moment. He wanted to make sure he had plenty of dimes so he could call everyone he knew. In addition to all of the baby announcement calls; he kept one special dime so he could call Rodney, his scalper friend, as soon as the Knick game ended, to tell him that if he ever gave him the finger like that again, he would fuckin' cut it off.

Vincent Morelli was able to fight through the holiday traffic to see the birth of his son. He made it just in time and he and Maryanne lay next to each other later that night with young Francis in their arms. Francis Michael Morelli was born at 4:16 pm on December 16, 1980. His parents called him Frankie.

WALLY McDOUGAL HAD PISSED MORE people off in Penn Station in one day than George Steinbrenner did when he fired Billy Martin. He pushed past hundreds of people, cursed out bartenders, and now he was after the guy who was selling newspapers. As he was trying to do his best to stay between the lines on the platform, screaming about his missing wallet, the sound of his obnoxious voice took the smile right off of Joe Mullaney's face. Joe had been the son of an alcoholic, so he knew drunken rage when he heard it.

Joe picked up his yellow Pony gym bag and began to walk in the direction of this voice.

"Where's the fuckin' news stand?" McDougal's voice was really escalating at this point. "These fuckin' immigrants, the guy probably stole the goddamn thing!"

People were backing away from this guy with each step he

took. Sweating, stinking of booze, with remnants of cocaine on the outsides of his nostrils, he spotted the exact news stand where he swore he left his wallet.

Joe Mullaney was about fifteen feet from McDougal and really just wanted to grab him, tell him to shut his mouth, and be on his way. He really didn't feel like missing the birth of his first child to deal with this prick. Little did he know what he was in for.

McDougal tried to avoid a briefcase that was on the ground on the platform. He slipped, and fell backwards. He slammed his head on the platform, then rolled like a heap of carnage onto the track.

The No. 2 train was bearing down on McDougal's lifeless body, the lights of the train quickly illuminating the white tile of the subway cave. Mullaney saw this happening and had already sprung into action. He leapt toward McDougal and dove on top of him, trying desperately to free him, as McDougal's arm was stuck on a sharp piece of metal. Joe Mullaney put both of his hands under McDougal's armpits and used every bit of strength that he had to free up his arm, and roll him over, off the track.

Mullaney was able to roll over onto his right shoulder, and was now lying underneath McDougal, exposing himself, as the train ripped through the station.

McDougal was saved, lying there, face up, atop broken bottles and rattraps. His head was bleeding like a sieve.

Joe wasn't so lucky. His left leg was struck. The train only dragged him a few feet, taking the severed part of his leg the rest of the way, leaving him behind.

When Joe Mullaney woke up that morning, he knew there was a good chance he was headed for the hospital that day. Never did he think it would be like this.

KATHY SAT AT THE WINDOW looking outside, and she began to get a bit worried. Joe promised her he would be on time that night to take her to the hospital. It was about 6:45 pm, and there was no sign of him. She phoned her neighbors next door but there was no answer. When she looked out the back window, she noticed the light on in Pete's garage. She grabbed her coat and headed for the back door.

When she walked next door across a thin sheet of ice, her skinny arms and legs tentatively balanced her protruding pregnant belly. A belly that looked like a basketball under a T-shirt contrasted against her lean lanky body. Kathy had long dirty-blonde hair, and greenish blue eyes.

She opened the garage door to find Pete, with a cloud of sanded-down dust behind him and a generator so loud he couldn't hear a word she said. He motioned to her with his index finger as if to say, "one sec," and he leaned toward the generator to shut it off.

"What's wrong?" Pete asked.

"I'm really worried. Joe got off work at four and should be here by now. He's never late, and if he is, he always calls."

She was so concerned about her husband at this point that she was not even timing her contractions. Kathy had a habit of twirling her hair when she was nervous. She had been twirling it for the past hour.

"Calm down, I'm sure he's fine. Did you call his job?"

"I called, but they said he left a while ago. This isn't like him, Pete." She began to cry.

Being the wife of a guy in this line of work is tough enough. You spend all day worried that something bad may happen while they're on duty, and usually begin to breathe your first sigh of relief when you know for sure that they are on their way home. Kathy Mullaney had a bad feeling, and the time between her contractions was getting shorter and shorter.

Pete quickly put down the mask he was wearing to prime a '71 Cutlass, threw down his gloves, and helped Kathy back into the house. Pete's wife had taken their five kids to the Corpus Christi Parish holiday party down the block, but Pete didn't go. He promised Joe he would stay home to make sure he would be around in case there was an emergency, never thinking there would actually be one.

"Okay Kathy, let's go." Pete rubbed his hand on Kathy's shoulder to console her. "I'll get the car." This was the sixth time around for Pete, but Kathy was a novice.

Kathy phoned her parents and told them to meet her at the hospital. She also called her friend, Laura Puma, and asked her to try to find out where Joe was. She told Laura to let Joe know that she went to the hospital with Pete and for him to meet them there. Kathy's contractions were less than five minutes apart.

"Take it easy, Kathy," said Pete, as he helped her into the passenger seat of the car. He shut the door and as he was running around to the driver's side, he was talking aloud with the winter frost shooting out of his mouth. "Please God, don't let this fuckin' water break." Pete was so worked up he was still wearing the fuckin' Jets helmet.

It was only three miles to Astoria General Hospital, but it felt like three hundred. As they were pulling into the hospital parking lot, Kathy was screaming in pain, and crying at the same time. She still had no idea where Joe was and it looked like this baby was not going to wait.

Transit Sergeant Ryan Ott was the first cop to arrive on the scene. He found Mullaney's identification in his gym bag by the tracks. After Sgt. Ott called Mullaney's office and found out that his wife was in labor, he called the 114th Precinct, which covers parts of Astoria, so they could arrange to have an officer inform Joe's wife of the news.

Kathy was headed into the delivery room, screaming in pain and crying for her husband. Screaming, interrupted by more and more crying and screaming. Pete was there every step of the way, but Joe was not.

IT WAS A FRIGID NIGHT and there was a Bellevue Hospital ambulance weaving in and out of cabs, cars, and buses, all the while, running red lights. The sirens were blaring and although people on the street really had no idea who was in that ambulance, they could sense the urgency. The ambulance pulled up to where a crew of nurses and doctors were waiting.

Wally McDougal was sitting in Triage, waiting for the two-inch gash above his left eye to be stitched. He was still drunk and was, no doubt, in for the fuckin' hangover of his life.

Rachael Pine just graduated from nursing school. This was her first day at Bellevue. She was twenty-two years old. Her face, full of freckles, was framed by very dark curly red hair. She couldn't believe the way McDougal was acting, as he was pacing back and forth with blood seeping through his gauze bandage.

"Hey nurse," said McDougal. "What's the story, when can I get the fuck outta here?"

Nurse Pine hesitated before answering him. "Not for a while, sir," said Pine. "You'll need stitches, and then it's up to the doctors to decide if they will keep you overnight."

The past few hours had been a blur to McDougal. Dr. James Mastaglio was a doctor in the ER for over ten years. He had sutured hundreds of patients over the years, but the stench of booze coming from this guy was so overpowering, he thought he might vomit. "You're a very lucky man, sir," said Dr. Mastaglio. "There's a man in surgery right now who was seriously injured trying to save your life. You would be dead if it wasn't for him. At least that's what I have been hearing."

McDougal responded. "I need a fuckin' cigarette, Doc. When is this shit gonna be over? Oh my fuckin' head. My wife is gonna fuckin' kill me."

McDougal was discharged about an hour later. He never asked about Mullaney, he was probably too drunk to even care. He stumbled out of the emergency room and hopped in a cab.

Joe Mullaney was undergoing emergency surgery. He lost massive amounts of blood.

KATHY'S PARENTS, JOHN AND PATRICIA O'Neill, came running into the delivery area of Astoria General. They were a good-looking couple, always impeccably dressed. John was about six-two, 180 pounds. He had dark curly hair and a mustache. Patricia was almost as tall as her husband. She had shoulder-length light brown hair, amber-colored eyes and a beauty mark on her right cheekbone that creased with her wide smile. Patricia was nervous. Kathy's friend Laura was waiting for them at the bank of elevators. They approached the first doctor they saw, who walked them down the hall into a private room where Kathy's obstetrician was waiting to speak to them. "What's wrong?" Patricia gasped. "Is it Kathy? Is it the baby?"

"No ma'am. Your daughter just gave birth to a beautiful baby boy and they're both fine."

John and Patricia were overjoyed and relieved. Two cops from the 114th waited outside while the O'Neill's were speaking with the doctor. When the doctor left, the officers came into the room to tell the O'Neill's what had happened to their son-in-law.

Sergeant Owen Farrell, an eighteen-year veteran, wanted the O'Neill's to know that Joe was in serious condition but he had survived this horrific accident. "Joe is alive, Mr. and Mrs. O'Neill," said Sgt. Farrell. "He's in critical condition at Bellevue. He jumped down from a subway platform onto the tracks and saved a man's life. He lost the lower portion of one of his legs." Nothing had prepared the O'Neill's for this news.

"Patricia, I'm going over to Bellevue with the officers," said John. "You stay here with Laura and I will call you at the nurses' station as soon as I know what the hell's going on with Joe." The O'Neill's were like parents to Joe. His mother and father were both deceased. It was important that he had his family with him at this time and John knew that.

John left Patricia with her head pressed against the glass window of the nursery looking at their grandson. As hard as she tried, she couldn't keep back the tears. It was surreal.

When John arrived at Bellevue, Joe was in Intensive Care. Chief Surgeon, Dr. Anthony Manno, was waiting to speak to John. The operation was successful. However, Joe lost a lot of blood and the damage to his arteries was extensive. He told John that in all probability, with intense physical therapy, that Joe would be able to function, using a cane. Dr. Manno did not think he would be confined to a wheelchair because the injury was below the kneecap. The news was bittersweet, but John knew it could have been much worse and was grateful just knowing that Joe was going to live.

After thirteen hours, Joe opened his eyes. He was drugged and exhausted. He looked up and saw his father-in-law. John smiled at him and asked, "Hey buddy, how ya feeling?"

"John?" asked Joe, with his eyes half opened and completely black and blue. "What the hell happened?"

"You had a little accident kid, but you're gonna be fine," said John.

"Hey John?"

"Yeah, pal?"

Joe Mullaney had no idea what kind of accident he had been involved in, but loving sports as much as he did, it didn't surprise John what came out of his mouth next. "Did the Knicks win tonight?"

"Yeah buddy," answered John, chuckling slightly, feeling so bad for this guy, knowing that Joe doesn't even know he's a dad yet, but happy they were having a conversation. "Yeah pal, they played great. They had the game on tape delay on Channel Two out in the hallway. I watched the whole thing."

The Knicks had actually gotten killed by the Philadelphia 76er's, but there was no way John was going to tell him that. Joe smiled and drifted back to sleep.

After several more hours, Dr. Manno came back to the waiting area looking for John. "Mr. O'Neill, your son-in-law is awake and he's asking about his wife."

Taking a deep breath, John said, "Thank God. Thanks so much, Dr. Manno. I'm gonna go tell him that Edward Joseph Mullaney has the bravest dad in the world."

Vinny Morelli was sitting at Pipin's Pub, an Irish bar, on Third Avenue, in Bay Ridge. His ass was half on and half off of his chair, as he leaned his elbows on the bar with his eyes glued to the television. He was chuckin' high fives around the bar anticipating the biggest score of his gambling career. Normally, he was a little more superstitious than he was acting tonight and wouldn't dare be caught up in an early celebration, but he just had a great feeling. He was finally gonna have his day. He had won every single game of the 1986 World Series that he bet, and everyone in the neighborhood knew about it. Boston was leading the series 3-2 and he was five for five so far, having bet the Red Sox for the over-all series as well. The Mets were heavy favorites in the series and Vinny really thought this was gonna be the bet of the century.

Vinny's wife, Maryanne, left him in 1983. She moved in with her boss, a high profile defense attorney from Long Island.

Vinny couldn't care less. He was making a ton of money right now; he was scalping World Series tickets, driving his cab, and he had been so hot with his gambling that he was on a natural high. He had his two kids, his son, Frankie, who was almost six, and a four-year-old daughter, Christina. Frankie looked exactly like his father. He was a good-looking Italian kid with slicked back brown hair and brown eyes. He was a southpaw with a great wiffle-ball curve ball, and despite his youth, was always picked first when the kids on his block were choosing teams for their street games. Christina looked just like her mom. She had big blue eyes and long, curly dark hair, with a few faint freckles across the bridge of her nose.

Vinny's kids both lived with him in his Brooklyn apartment, but he wanted all of that to change. He was determined to get them out of there. Despite his bad habits, deep down, he tried to be a good guy. He had a hot temper but a soft side as well, and he really loved his kids.

"As soon as this fuckin' game ends that's it, Coach! This game is gonna buy us our house on Long Island, and then that's it, I'm out, no more gamblin'!"

Ray Fox, the bartender, who was better known by the locals as "Coach," looked Vinny square in the face and laughed. "Whatever you say, Vinny."

Coach Fox had been working at Pipin's for seventeen years and he'd seen and heard it all before. He was a former Little League baseball coach in the area and a sports writer for the local paper, covering all of the kids' sporting events in Bensonhurst and Bay Ridge. Coach had a regular crowd that would come and visit him at the bar every time he worked behind the stick. He was about five-eight with thinning gray hair and glasses. This was not the first time he had heard the old "This is my last bet" bullshit from Vinny.

"Remember North Carolina State, asshole?" asked Coach. "My boy Valvano was dancing around like a fuckin' lunatic, looking for someone to hug, and you were looking for someone to kill. That was gonna be your last time too. I had to sit through that tirade and drive you to the hospital when you put your hand through my wall." Coach Fox was laughing a bit, but still looking to get his point across to Vinny. "I never got the money for my wall and I got stuck in the goddamn emergency room until four am! Don't pull any of that bullshit if these fuckin' Beantown assholes lose, you hear me?"

"Oh relax, Coach, it's a fuckin' lock," said Vinny, as he ordered another Dewar's and soda.

All the people in the bar were rooting for the Mets, except for Vinny and the few Yankee fans who were out that night. Every single Met fan was dressed in Met colors and they were just hoping for any sign of life from their team. The bar was packed. Maximum occupancy in Pipin's was a hundred people. This particular night, they were way over the limit. Vinny was loud. Really loud. He was rubbing it in bad. The Mets were trailing 5-3 in the top of the tenth inning. Dave Henderson of the Red Sox, just led off the inning with a home run off Rick Aguilera, and Marty Barrett drove in Wade Boggs later in the inning for what appeared to be the insurance run for the Sox. The Met fans in the bar were miserable. Maggie Cooney, a Pipin's regular, and loyal Mets season ticket holder, made the ultimate sacrifice, and gave her two tickets to Game 6 to her favorite nephews, Michael and Thomas, as their birthday present. She felt that if she wasn't going to be at Shea on this night, that being at her neighborhood pub was the next best thing. She was dressed just like *Mr. Met*, the team mascot, and she

31

was gripping her bottle of Miller Lite harder and harder each time Vinny cheered for the Red Sox.

Vinny was banging his hands on the bar, screaming and whistling. Any other guy would have gotten his head kicked in, but there were just too many people afraid of Vinny. He once reached over the counter of an OTB and tried to strangle the teller when he neglected to box his two-dollar exacta.

Calvin Schiraldi was now on the mound for the Sox. He had come into the game in the eighth inning and was still out there for the tenth. He retired Wally Backman and Keith Hernandez, on fly balls, for the first two outs of the inning.

"Buy all these fuckin' assholes a drink, and pour yourself a shot of tequila, Coach," yelled Vinny. "Go ahead, swallow the fuckin' worm, I'll buy you another one!"

Vinny was slamming his glass on the bar and there were ice cubes popping all over the place. He was yelling at the Met players as the camera flashed to them in the dugout. "Start polishing your fuckin' golf clubs, assholes. Your season is over!" He was looking around at all of the Met fans in the pub and screaming in their faces. "I hate the Mets, you hear me? I fuckin' hate them!"

On a 2-1 pitch Gary Carter hit a line drive single to left field, and Vinny began to quiet down, just slightly. Speaking out loud but not really yelling this time, Vinny said, "Come on Schiraldi, you only pitched three innings for Christ's sake, what are you fuckin' kiddin' me?"

Vinny was a little scared, but still didn't think anything this tragic could happen. The Red Sox were one out away from their first World Series title since 1918, and Vinny felt there was no way this could cave in now.

Steve Orr, a cousin of one of the regulars, who was about

twenty-one years old, leapt up on the bar and grabbed the old, yellowish, smoke-stained 1969 Mets banner off the wall above the bar. He was waving it in the air, avoiding any eye contact with Vinny, but being cheered by everyone wearing orange and blue. Vinny couldn't stand the fuckin' guy, but last year Orr helped him move a lot of his phony Ice Capades tickets for some guy from Williamsburg. This kid scammed a ton of people for Vinny. Each time Orr cheered for the Mets, Vinny just tried to ignore him because he needed him.

The Met fans were going insane. As Kevin Mitchell came to the plate to pinch-hit for Aguilera, Vinny pulled the bottom of his St. John's Redmen sweatshirt up to his face and started to bite down on the bottom of the shirt. He put one of his addias shell-top sneakers up on the bar and yelled, "One shoe, one shoe, come on Schiraldi you mutha fucka, one shoe."

Some of the Brooklyn Ranger fans the year before used to take off a shoe for good luck. Why Vinny was doing it now was anyone's guess, considering it obviously never worked for the Rangers in the playoffs. The cameras at the stadium were capturing tight shots of Met fans in warm jackets and Met hats, as their breath was shooting out of their mouths, chanting "Let's go Mets!"

The volume on the pub's television was at full blast. The Mets already had thirty-nine come-from-behind wins that year. The fans were thinking "Could there be a fortieth?" Vin Scully was doing the play-by-play, as Schiraldi delivered to Mitchell.

"Curve ball, and that's gonna be hit to center, base hit," yelled Scully. The bar was going wild. Vinny's eyes were starting to fill up as he was now officially scared shit. All he could think about were his kids, the house he wanted to buy on Long Island, and what a hero he'd be if he could just win this last time. He won $17,000 in the past month. Earlier in the month, he hit a monster triple at OTB, on three long shots, and won $6,500. He bet the entire amount on the Red Sox for the series. He needed them to win the series for him to win. He also bet each individual game and hit every single one. He was five-for-five so far with the Sox leading 3-2. He bet the Sox in the games they won, and the Mets in the two games they won. All of his scalping profits made during this World Series, $4,200, were placed on this game, Game 6.

Benny Tarangelo, a local paperboy and avid Met fan, was peeking in the window of Pipin's with a few of his friends by his side. The kid couldn't have been more than thirteen, but had enough balls to sneak in the back door so he could catch the end of the game. In fact, he was even given the nickname, "Balls," by his pals, for all of the stunts he had pulled. He grabbed an old towel in the back of the pub and walked around, posing as a fuckin' busboy, picking up empty glasses and shit. The crowd was too busy yelling in Vinny's face to notice the little nut. The kid was staring at Vinny and was shocked by the desperation in his eyes. He had never seen a gambler's angst before.

Vinny was starting to sweat under his acrylic sweatshirt, and there was a reminiscent tightness in his chest that he usually felt when he was staring up at an OTB television screen awaiting the results of a *photo finish*. Thoughts were racing through his mind of his huge down payment for his beautiful $97,000 house on Long Island. He started to speak, but nobody could hear him. They were all too busy cheering.

"Valley Stream, New York, Valley Stream, come on, come on, Schiraldi, you scumbag, take me to fuckin' Valley Stream baby! Come on, come on, come on, strike this son-of-a-bitch out you mutha fucka!" Ray Knight had an 0-2 count on him. "One more strike you son-of-a-bitch, one more!"

One hundred and fifty Pipin's patrons were transfixed on the Pub's twenty-four inch television screen as the ball left Knight's bat, blooping into the outfield, everyone praying that it's going to fall in for a base hit. Everyone, but Vinny. "And that's gonna be into center field, base hit!" yelled Scully, with almost disbelief in his voice. "Here comes Carter to score, and the tying run is at third in Kevin Mitchell."

Shea was literally shaking from left to right due to this incredible, yet characteristic, comeback by the renamed, "Miracle Mets," a name given to the organization after the 1969 World Series victory. They were in miracle range again and Vinny just kept his head down on the bar, feeling like he was going to vomit. His entire life savings was in the hands of Bob Stanley, who had just come in to replace Schiraldi. The Mets had runners at first and third, two outs, and Mookie Wilson had two strikes on him after fouling off a 2-1 pitch, bringing the Red Sox to within one strike of the World Series, yet again. Mookie fouled off the next pitch, and the one after that. Stanley's seventh pitch to Wilson went wild, and Mitchell was able to score the tying run. "And it's gonna go to the backstop, here comes Mitchell to score the tying run, and Ray Knight is at second base" yelled Scully. Knight was the winning run and in scoring position.

Vinny ordered his ninth Dewar's and soda. The repetitious kicking motion he was making along the pub's brass bar at his feet was starting to leave indentations that no one would ever see, but they were there. Steve Orr had the vintage banner wrapped around his head and he was jumping up and down. "Let's go Mets!" chants were deafening. With the count 3-2,

Wilson fouled the next pitch back. He then fouled the next pitch past third base. Bob Stanley, the Red Sox right-hander, had four chances to put Wilson away and Wilson fouled off each and every ball, staging a ten pitch at bat.

Mookie hit a ground ball down the first base line. Bill Buckner, the Sox first baseman, with a history of chronic knee and ankle problems, began to stagger slightly when the ball made its way toward him, and Vin Scully made the famous call. "A little roller up along first....behind the bag....it gets through Buckner! Here comes Knight....and the Mets win it!"

Vinny couldn't hear Scully's call, the place was too loud and everyone was blocking his view, as all of the other patrons moved closer and closer to the TV. Vinny clutched his drink with his left hand and his chest with his right. He turned to Coach Fox and asked "Is it foul?" Vinny got his answer, but not from Coach. He looked up and over the cheering bar fans, and saw Ray Knight making his way around third, with his arms flailing in the air like a windmill. Knight placed his hands on the top of his helmet as he crossed the plate and was mobbed by the rest of his team. The Mets had forced a Game 7.

Vinny walked home that night with his right hand covered in blood. After sparing Coach Fox and his customers his hot temper, he decided to launch his hand through the window of a '72 Dodge Challenger parked three blocks down from the bar. He could hear the cheers coming from all of the Brooklyn houses as he made his way home. He was pissed off, drunk, and had no idea where to turn next. When he got home, he paid the babysitter with whatever he had left in his pocket, kissed his kids goodnight, leaving spots of blood on each of their pillows, and went to bed. He went to sleep that night, already planning his tactics for Game 7. "I'll get it back," he said.

Joe Mullaney took his usual post at Shea Stadium on October 27, 1986. He got a sweet deal as an usher about a year or two after his accident. He loved his job there. He was a die-hard Met fan and he saw every single home game for free. He got paid to watch his favorite team play and he loved it. Joe was assigned to work the handicapped section of the stadium. He had an extra soft spot for anyone with a disability, and working there made him realize how lucky he was to be able to stand up straight, even if he was only able to stand on one leg. This was *his* area. He never missed a game.

The fans who sat there loved him and their seats were right behind home plate. Joe would find himself always having to tell people to move along, making sure that all of the handicapped people were comfortable for each pitch. He knew everyone there — from the people who would catch a few games a year, to the blue collar season ticket holders who just loved their team, to the suits who sat in the corporate boxes, who Joe had always referred to as "shrimp-eaters," the white-collar dudes who thought they were hot shit, and would show up each night spending their company's money pounding beers and eating nothing but shrimp cocktails up in the Diamond Club.

Everyone loved "Joe the Cop," a nickname people still called him, even though he had not been on the job in six years.

Crowds were starting to roll in, still riled up from the incredible game they had witnessed two nights before. The field was still soaked from all of the rain that had fallen a day earlier, postponing Game 7 until tonight. The few Boston fans in the crowd still looked crestfallen. The pain of Game 6 remained.

Joe was excited. He was looking nervously at his watch, waiting for Kathy and their two kids to arrive. His team had a shot to win the World Series and they were going to be able to see it, together. Tom Chimera, one of his favorite "shrimp-eaters," who had seats down in a box five rows off of the field, had to go out of town for business and gave his box for Game 7 to Joe so his family could see the game.

Eddie had seen a few games before, but never a World Series game. Eddie was getting big. He was nearly six-years-old and had a full head on the rest of the kids in his class. His reddish hair and freckles melded with his green eyes to make for a perfect map of Ireland. Joe's five-year-old daughter, Colleen, was making her professional baseball game debut at Game 7 of the 1986 World Series. She had blonde curly hair peaking out from under an oversized Met cap, freckles and big brown eyes opened wide as she waited for her favorite team to take the field.

More than fifty thousand Met fans were disappointed by the second inning. Ron Darling let up three runs when Dwight Evans and Rich Gedman blasted back-to-back home runs and Boggs hit an RBI single. Sox pitcher, Bruce Hurst, was on his way to his third win of the series, after having won games one and five, until the Mets did it again. The Mets would go on to win the game 8-5 for their first World Series title since 1969. Red Sox great, Wade Boggs, sat in the dugout crying, and the Met fans left Flushing chanting, "Let's go Mets!" loud enough to be heard in Boston.

FRANKIE MORELLI WAS SO EXCITED to be receiving his First Holy Communion. Frankie was slick. He sometimes dressed like he earned a decent living. He was only six years old, but played the part of someone a lot older whenever he got the chance. He was one of those neighborhood kids who, despite his nasty mouth, was liked by all the parents, they just didn't want their kids talking like him.

Today was Frankie's big day. All the kids love this day. The excitement of that first big party where everyone comes to honor them, handing them envelopes full of money was something Frankie could hardly wait for.

Frankie's grandparents, Rose and Vincenzo Morelli, came to live with them a couple of months after their mother left. Vinny needed the help since he spent twelve hours a day driving a cab, and his nights gambling, scalping tickets, and running from guys to whom he owed money. Vincenzo and Rose told the kids that the reason why they were living with them was because their dad was very busy trying to start up his own cab service. Vinny's parents knew he was up to no good, but they did their best to cover for him. In Vinny's crazy mind, though, all of the things that he was doing were just to try to provide a better life for his kids. Frankie didn't mind the crowded Brooklyn apartment. His grandparents took good care of him and he knew he could count on them for a few extra bucks on his Communion.

Vinny's parents were both in their seventies. They were hard-working people who knew the value of a dollar. Even though they spoke with heavy Sicilian accents, they had no trouble communicating with their grandkids. They owned a deli down the block from the apartment where Vincenzo put in long hours. Rose did most of the cooking, and together they managed to keep their heads above water.

"I'm gonna make a bundle today Christina," said Frankie, when he got to the table for breakfast, knowing that all he was getting was a glass of tap water. He was awaiting the taste of the Host for the first time that day, and wasn't permitted to eat before mass.

His grandmother quickly jumped in and said, "Frankie, the mosta important thing is you' family will be here to a see you make you' Communion and that a you' be able to receive Jesus every Sunday from a now a on."

Frankie slicked his hair back with the palm of his left hand.

His grandmother continued. "If you' lucky to get a few dollars, you' have to try to sava' every dime so one day you' can go to a college," she proclaimed. "Thatza what today is about."

"No Nonna, today is about my new Nike sneakers and a talking Cabbage Patch Kid for Christina. I'm not saving anything Nonna, I am going shopping tomorrow and I am spending as much of it as I can before daddy finds it and loses it."

Frankie always had money and he never told his father about it. He would help old ladies home from the store, or help the teenagers in the neighborhood fold their newspapers. He would do anything to try to make a buck.

Frankie knew at a young age that his dad was a compulsive gambler and he swore he would never let himself get that way. He loved his dad very much and figured that he would just get lucky one day and all of his problems would go away. The kid hated seeing his father running away from people he owed money, and he would see it way too often. His dad took him to Opening Day at Yankee Stadium about a month earlier. Vinny got the fuckin' beatin' of his life from a couple of loan sharks outside the bowling alley by the right field bleacher entrance of the stadium. Frankie saw the whole thing.

Frankie was dressed in a white suit standing in the hallway of his apartment waiting for the sound of the church bells from St. Leo's. Frankie and Christina's church and school were adjacent brick edifices built sometime in the early 1900's. It was a beautiful day in May, with only a few sparse clouds strewn across the sky. Frankie was relieved that the weather was nice. His obsession with money was abnormal at his age. He knew that the nicer the weather, the more cash he'd make because the more people would show up.

Nicky Ventimiglia, Frankie's neighbor, and best friend from school, was also making his First Communion. Nicky was really small for his age, standing three feet tall with greasy hair and a saliva-stained cowlick on the right side of his head.

Frankie and Nicky were never apart, and Nicky's mom always had a soft spot for Frankie and Christina, knowing they suffered because of Vinny's gambling. Frankie was happy that she thought to combine the parties because the Morelli apartment was too small.

Marguerite Ventimiglia, Nicky's mom, was a widow at the age of forty-two. She was a pretty woman, with light reddish-brown hair, and blue eyes. Her husband, Nick, was tragically killed the year before in a freak accident when the axle on his van snapped in half as he was working his bread route on Flatbush Ave. He struck a utility pole and was killed instantly. Marguerite was devastated by the loss of her husband, but she stayed strong for her son, Nicky, and her two daughters. She made sure she kept a positive attitude for them and always kept the back door open for the Morelli kids as well.

The crowd came rolling into the Ventimiglia's and Frankie looked like a mini John Travolta on the *Saturday Night Fever* album cover. Everything was white: the shirt, the tie, the suit, the shoes, and even the little prayer book that the nuns gave out. So were all of the envelopes. You could see the look on Frankie's face as his guests were handing him his gifts. He had all kinds of shit going through his head as he reached out to grab each envelope. These cards could have read *Congrats on your Communion, Asshole.* It didn't matter. Frankie took no time to read them. He never held that much money in his life, and he couldn't wait to blow it.

You could see his face and read his mind. *New sneaks, Knick jacket, doll for Christina, Winfield jersey, Yankee tickets for me and Dad, new glove, new bike.*

Most kids would just give the cards to their parents. Not Frankie. In fact, his friend Nicky walked over to him as he was tossing yet another Communion card in the garbage after grabbing the money and adding it to the wad of money in his pocket. Nicky had a look of confusion on his face.

"Why don't you give that money to your dad, Frankie? This way you won't lose it."

"Fuck that, Nicky, this money is staying right here in my pocket," snapped Frankie.

On one of the holiest and most special days in a Catholic kid's life, this second grader was protecting his money. The kid was walking around with his pockets filled with tens and twenties.

Later that night, when the party ended and everyone went home, Frankie made his way to the little shoebox he kept under his bed in his room with a wad of money totaling $840. He had already planned out the next day. He was going to go with his grandmother and Christina to the mall with $300 of the $840. A deal his grandmother coaxed him into making, in an effort to start a college fund.

The next day came and they all headed for the mall. Frankie had a hundred bucks in his right sneaker and a hundred in his left sneaker. He had fifty bucks in his right pocket and the other fifty in his left. This was something he had seen his father do a million times. His dad never did it because he was afraid he was going to get mugged. He always figured, if a shylock got him, he wouldn't have to give up all his cash at once.

Frankie had the day of his life. He bought Christina a top-of-the-line Cabbage Patch Doll, one that could talk. He bought himself a beautiful pair of the new Air Jordan sneakers, a Knick jacket, Knick bag, and a white Ranger jersey. He bought his grandma a grocery carriage with wheels to assist her with her shopping. He even knew enough to buy Mrs. Ventimiglia some flowers to thank her for allowing his family to use their home. The thing he was most excited about was the gift he got for his dad. Don Mattingly was his father's favorite Yankee at the time. He bought his dad one of those blue long-sleeve sweatshirts with the Yankee *NY* logo in the upper left hand corner. He had the man at the sweatshirt shop sew his dad's initials above the logo and Mattingly's number twenty-three below it. He was so excited to surprise his father with it.

When he opened up the door to his room to put his change back under his bed, he saw his shoebox out on the floor between his bed and Christina's, knowing that he did not leave it there.

His father had stolen his Communion money, leaving behind a note for Frankie that read: *I took the money to buy you something special buddy, I'll give it back to you by Friday pal. I love you….Love Daddy.* Frankie knew this was bullshit, and he cried himself to sleep, using his dad's new sweatshirt as a blanket.

THE MULLANEY FAMILY FILED OUT of St. Francis R.C. Church. They were so proud that Eddie had just received his First Holy Communion. Eddie was walking down the steps of the church, all smiles, staring at Eydie Collins, the girl that his teacher, Sister Benedict, paired him up with during the procession. Eydie was staring back at him. Like all the girls at school, she loved Eddie, even at their young age. He was a star in all of the local sports, the first kid to go off the diving board at the Surf Club, the strongest kid in the grade, and the smartest kid in the class. The math problems they were doing at St. Francis were things like $7 \times 7 = 49$. When Sister Benedict had the kids turn to these pages in their workbooks, it literally made him laugh. He'd finish two or three pages before the rest of the class had two or three problems done.

Joe purchased a video recorder so he could record the Mass.

Some folks had never even seen one of these before, much less owned one. Joe saved a few bucks and bought the best camera he could find with the help of *Consumer Reports Magazine.*

Joe was a conservative guy who had some rough years but always provided for his family and always made sure that his kids got most of the things they desired, within reason. He pretended to let his daughter, Colleen, help him with the camera when the kids started walking out of the church.

Eddie couldn't wait for his party. Kathy and Joe invited every one of Eddie's friends, all of his cousins, and his aunts and uncles. They had an eighteen by thirty foot tent set up, covering the entire yard in case it rained. Luckily the weather was great that day, so they didn't even need it.

Eddie's favorite aunt, Auntie Joan, would come from Ireland each year to spend the summers with the Mullaney's. She flew in a month earlier that year to surprise Eddie. She was an elegant woman with dark hair, green eyes, and a slight brogue. Eddie loved the money cards that he was getting all day from his guests, but the gift that he loved most of all, was an autographed Darryl Strawberry baseball that he got from his Auntie Joan.

Eddie knew exactly how he was going to allocate his money. He had a list of his guests up in his room on his desk and he wanted to make sure that he sent his thank you cards out the very next day.

He had three different beat-up wallets on his desk: brown, tan and black. They were hand-me-downs from his father. The first one was labeled "Schwinn Hurricane 5." This was the bike that he really wanted desperately and his dad told him that he would pay half if Eddie paid the other half.

The second wallet was labeled "Independence Savings," the

neighborhood bank, where Eddie was going to open his first bank account with his parents.

The last wallet read "Eddie's Race Horse." The Mullaney's moved out of Woodside shortly after Colleen was born, and now lived in the Marine Park section of Brooklyn, a few miles from Rockaway Beach. Kathy's two sisters lived there and she wanted to be closer to them. Joe had taken Eddie and Colleen horseback riding a few weeks before, near Jamaica Bay, where there was a huge riding stable. Eddie had been going there for years, petting and feeding the horses. Once he got a chance to ride one, all he wanted to do was own one. His father asked him what he wanted for his Communion and he said that he would like to go out to Belmont and bet on the horse races with his money. That never happened, but he thought it was worth a try.

Eddie received over one thousand dollars on his big day, and the savings had begun.

Vinny headed towards Aqueduct Racetrack in Queens; with what was left of Frankie's Communion money. He would normally do most of his wagering at the local OTB in Brooklyn, but he was really on the run at this point. He had some bad fuckin' people chasing him, and he was way too afraid to hang around his own neighborhood. He felt so guilty, but he was determined to make it up to Frankie. He had already prepared his bullshit story for Frankie. He was going to tell him that he got a great deal on some season tickets for the Yankees, and he had to get them right away, so he was just borrowing the money until he got paid at the cabstand.

Vinny looked at every race on that day's card. He needed a win and he needed one bad. Between the World Series, the ponies, and the NBA playoffs, this compulsive train-wreck was on the hook for over thirty grand.

He used about ten or twelve different bookies throughout Brooklyn and the Bronx over the past six months. He tried to spread out his action so that each bookmaker thought they had only been dealing with a small amount of money. He was maxed out everywhere. There was nobody left to take his action. The horses were his only option.

Most of his bookie bets had been paid off by a low-level loan shark named Fuzzy McGlynn from Bensonhurst. Vinny had done a few scams for him before; scalping tickets to games, selling a few phony Rolex watches, that kind of shit. McGlynn was about six-one with light brown hair and a beard without the mustache. His arms were like steel pipes and he had a tattoo of a shamrock on his neck. His hands were as rough as sandpaper and his knuckles were fully scabbed. His eyebrows were bright blonde and he looked as if he had been sunbathing at the fuckin' Equator. His face was beet red.

Knowing Vinny's reputation, Fuzzy didn't trust him with money at all. He made sure that he escorted Vinny to each and every person who he owed money, so he could settle each debt, personally. Fuzzy paid off just about every single guy who had been chasing Vinny around, except for a guy named Nino Grilli, Vinny's good friend from high school, whom Vinny bet with from time to time. Nino told Vinny to get his fuckin' life straight first, and then he'd start him on a payment plan for the three grand he owed him, probably figuring that he'd never get the fuckin' money back, but feeling bad enough to give him a chance. Fuzzy settled the rest of Vinny's debts, and Vinny's ass belonged to him now.

Fuzzy McGlynn didn't like not being paid back. Most of all, he despised being ignored. He wasn't all that busy loaning people money, mostly because people were just too afraid to borrow it from him. He had one main customer right now and that was Vinny. Fuzzy was a career criminal who had done time in a slew of New York State prisons, and was a suspect in two unsolved murders in the Bronx. He was also a well-known drug and gun dealer in East New York. He wasn't afraid to take action if a guy couldn't pay. He would rather just wipe the guy out so he'd be rid of the hassle.

McGlynn sat in the back of a white 1985 Cutlass Supreme, with a loaded .38 caliber pistol on the floor of the car between his feet. His friend John Abruzzo, who lived in Mount Vernon, was driving the car doing his best to keep up with Vinny who was weaving in and out of the Sunday drivers on the Belt Parkway, trying like hell to make the first race.

Abruzzo was the equivalent of a "sweat-hog." He wasn't too swift, and pretty much did as he was told. He tried to be tough, but he just didn't have it. He was about five-seven with pinkie rings on each hand and curly black hair. He was a gangster wannabe, but he wasn't even close. He would try to recite lines from *The Godfather* when he confronted various people and they just fuckin' laughed at him. Half the time he got the fuckin' lines wrong anyway. He was so stupid, and the perfect puppet for Fuzzy.

These guys were following Vinny for days and knew that he would never be able to repay his debt. This left them with only one choice. They'd much rather whack him back in Brooklyn, where they knew the neighborhood and had a shot at making a clean getaway. They still hadn't decided if they would wait for him to get all the way back to Brooklyn, or get him when he left Aqueduct and dump him by Kennedy Airport.

Abruzzo noticed Vinny's car start to slow down on the Belt. Vinny made his way to the side of the parkway; there was smoke shooting from the hood.

"Oh, this is too good to be true Fuz, this fuckin' guy is over-heatin', let's just do a drive-by and get the hell outta here," said Abruzzo, pulling his car off to the side of the parkway about twenty car lengths back.

"Relax," said McGlynn. "This degenerate asshole owes me twenty-seven grand, and there is no fuckin' way we're getting him now."

"What are we gonna do?" asked Abruzzo.

"We'll wait until he has one last day with the ponies. We'll grab him and check his pockets. If he hits a race or two, and he's got like a grand or more on him, we'll take it, and let him live another day."

Abruzzo cracked his knuckles listening to the plan.

"If he's broke and cryin' like a fuckin' baby, like he usually is, I'm gonna shoot him right there on the spot, fuck 'em!" said McGlynn.

Abruzzo really didn't agree with this idea. He wanted to whack Vinny on the run and go home. He was just too weak to object to McGlynn's plan.

"I got an idea," said McGlynn. "I'm getting out here and walking to the track."

"What? You can't do that, it's too far, what are you nuts?" exclaimed Abruzzo. "We don't even…"

"Shut up! I know what I'm doing," yelled McGlynn. "The track is about two miles down. He knows what I look like, but he has no idea who you are. You wait until this desperate ass-hole starts flagging people down, and if I know this guy, that will be sooner than later. Pull up to him and just ask him if he needs a lift somewhere."

"Yeah but what if he says…." Abruzzo tried to speak but

was cut off by McGlynn once again.

"He's not gonna say no. I know this guy, he has to make that first race! He's a fuckin' loser, believe me. This guy once gambled on two finalists in a fuckin' water balloon toss at a block party," McGlynn said. "Just ask him if he needs a lift, and when he says yes, which he will do, don't say a word about the track, not a fuckin' word. Let him do all of the talking, you got it?"

"Got it," said Abruzzo, with some hesitation in his voice, but fully ready to do as McGlynn asked.

"After you drop him off, don't let him out of your sight. Let him go inside and watch where he goes in. Wherever he ends up, will probably be where he stays for the day, or at least until he loses all of his fuckin' money." McGlynn continued, "As you know and I know, horse gamblers don't head out to the actual track to watch the race, they like the televisions. Most of the TVs are on the main floor, so that's where he'll be. Meet me outside right by the finish line as soon as the second race ends. That should give me enough time to get there."

McGlynn exited the car and walked up the side of the Parkway. He found a hole in the fence just before the Cross Bay Blvd exit. His loaded gun was tucked in his belt under his Lee denim jacket and sweatshirt. He ducked his body through the fence hole and made his way towards the racetrack, realizing with each block he passed, that no matter what, he had to kill Vinny. A chase this intense had to have a beneficial ending.

Vinny started to wave his hands in the air as the cars were whizzing by. Abruzzo pulled his car off of the parkway right behind Vinny's. He got out and started to walk around to the front of Vinny's yellow 1977 Pontiac Firebird that he had just purchased a week before from his neighbor, Tommy Bridgette, with money he really didn't have. He gave Bridgette a fuckin' rubber check and fifty singles, hoping he could lay low for a while before the guy came looking for him. There was smoke shooting out of the car like a fuckin' volcano and Vinny was flippin' out.

"What'd ya overheat there, pal?" asked Abruzzo, sticking his head under the hood and standing next to Vinny.

Vinny backed away from the hood of the car and was running his fingers through his hair in a very nervous manner. He was desperate and he was way more concerned with the first race than his piece of shit car. He'd walk back to Brooklyn if he had to, as long as he could catch a few races. He really had his eye on that first race. He loved the number seven horse, *Candy Apple Addie,* and the morning line was 8-1. He had to get there.

"Which way you headed?" asked Abruzzo.

Vinny was desperate. He needed to get to the track. He had that "sure thing" in the first race and post time was in seven minutes. "I'm going over to the racetrack, ya mind giving me a lift?"

"Not at all, hop in," said Abruzzo.

"Where ya from?" asked Vinny, not really caring if the guy was from the fuckin' moon, just hoping that he would get him to Aqueduct quickly.

"I'm from Westchester," said Abruzzo. "But my mom lives over in Valley Stream and I'm just heading out to see her. She lives by herself, so I try to get down there at least once a week, just to check in on her."

You could see the envy in Vinny's degenerate gambling eyes. Valley Stream was a very affordable place to live. That's the place he had dreamed of buying a house for his family.

One of his cabbie buddies, "Pebble Head" Beissel, lived there for years and told Vinny about it a while back. Here he was, with his kid's Communion money split between the soles of his left and right Pro-Ked sneakers, trying to get even on the very money he had lost trying to purchase a house in that same town, and the guy driving the car was only there for one reason — to help Fuzzy McGlynn kill him. The irony was as thick as Vinny's New York accent.

Abruzzo dropped Vinny off right in front of the Clubhouse entrance. Vinny was happy, this guy just saved him a few minutes and he needed every second.

"Take care," said Abruzzo, as he stopped the car for Vinny to get out. "Good luck today!"

Vinny slammed the door behind him, and ran right into the track. When he got inside, he looked up at one of the TVs and saw that post time was in one minute. He sprinted to a betting window and got on the back of the line. He had to bet the seven horse and the line was moving way too slow. The minimum at this window was fifty dollars per wager, and was usually not as crowded as the other windows, but today, all the lines were long.

He was on line with six other people in front of him, and he started to yell out loud "Come on, come on!" He was petrified that he wouldn't make it. He looked at the board and saw that the odds had gone up to 12-1. This was a six-furlong allowance race on a fast track. The horse he liked missed his last three starts due to an infection in his right foot. Before that, he finished second in a $150,000 Stakes Race at Belmont. Nobody was betting him because they were all too afraid of that injury. Earlier in the week, Vinny drove the horse's trainer, Bo Spinner, in his cab. Bo said that the injury wasn't bad, and that the horse was a fuckin' "gorilla in the barn" that couldn't wait to break out.

"Gorilla in the barn" is a phrase that an Irish guy, Brian Dunn, from Park Slope, would scream every time he thought a horse was a sure thing. Dunn single-handedly coined that phrase, and if you listen closely, as you walk through any of the NYRA racetracks, you'll hear people screaming the funny catchphrase before any big race. Vinny was fearing that his "gorilla" was gonna fuckin' take off without him getting his bet in, and he was starting to scream his fuckin' head off as they loaded the first of nine horses into the gate. He was yelling at the guy in front of him, "Ya have to know who the fuck you're gonna bet man, come on! Ya can't be readin' your fuckin' program at the window!"

People on the other lines were staring at Vinny. He was dressed in a flannel shirt with a pack of Camels in his pocket, gray sweat pants, and he was slapping his racing form against his leg. "Hurry up!" he screamed.

The man in front of him finished and Vinny stepped up.

"Five Hundred to win on the seven!"

Vinny looked up at the monitor and saw the last horse being loaded into the gate. He panicked and bit down on his knuckles.

"Please get the bet in, please!" Vinny cried.

The quick-fingered teller at the window got the bet in, just in time. Vinny ran away with his ticket in his hand, looking for a bigger TV. Six furlongs is a short race and Vinny knew it would be over soon. As the horses made the turn at the top of the stretch there were two horses that were way ahead of the rest of the field and one of them was the seven.

"Come on, you mutha fucka, one time, one time you son-of-a-bitch, come on, come on!" The three and the seven were battling, neither horse giving in, the jockeys on each horse, changing their whips from the right side to the left, trying to win this race. The seven horse won by a neck!

Vinny just won over six grand and the thoughts of that house on Long Island were running around in his head again. He gathered himself and took a seat on a bench. After about twenty minutes he began to thumb through his program frantically.

He started to talk to himself, trying to catch his breath. "Whew. Wow, holy shit. Okay, Vinny, relax," he said to himself. "The number two and the number six in the second race, are *much the best*. I'm fuckin' boxin' them, because if I bet it *cold* and it comes in the other way, I'll fuckin' faint."

"Okay, let's see," said Vinny, as he was breathing heavy, thumbing through his racing form. The number two horse is 5-2 and the number six horse is 2-1. He continued to speak to himself. "The least that exacta will pay if I box it is about sixteen or eighteen bucks." He looked up at the board. There was five minutes until post time.

Vinny hadn't eaten since the day before at Frankie's party, and he was starving. He turned toward the pretzel stand, and saw the guy that had just picked him up on the side of the Belt Parkway, standing there eating a pretzel and drinking a Coke. He knew this was no coincidence. He knew that he must have been followed.

"I gotta get the fuck outta here man!" Vinny said to himself. "Shit, I still gotta cash this fuckin' ticket."

He ran to a different window at the opposite end of the track, closer to the exit, put the ticket on the counter, and awaited the look on the teller's face. "Whoa," said the teller, when the total came up. "Congrats, sir! You won $6,360.00." Vinny was fully aware that he didn't have to pay taxes on the money he was about to collect. As long as the winnings don't exceed 600-1 odds, then he didn't have to tell Uncle Sam a fuckin' thing. He knew there would be no forms to fill out, but he was still pressed for time, fully aware that Fuzzy was close by.

"Thanks, can you please hurry," said Vinny, looking over his shoulder.

"Okay, take it easy. It's gonna take me a while to count that money, sir" said the teller.

The teller counted up to $6,200, all in hundred dollar bills. Vinny grabbed the money. "That's cool, I'm good, you keep the rest" leaving a hundred and sixty in the guy's hand and dashing for the door, splitting half of the pile of money between his pockets. He kept looking over his shoulders for the parkway guy.

"How could I be so fuckin' stupid?" Vinny said to himself. "I should have known that fuckin' roadside rescue was too good to be true and I was able to make the first race! God damn am I in trouble."

He raced through the parking lot of the track heading for the exit. He spotted a man standing at what appeared to be a bus stop on Rockaway Blvd, the main road that leads into the track. He ran straight for it, hoping to catch the next bus, having no idea where it was headed.

The man at the bus stop was facing the other way with the hood of his sweatshirt cinched all the way up. He turned towards Vinny. Vinny's eyes bolted out if his head. It was Fuzzy McGlynn.

Vinny got down on his knees and begged McGlynn for more time to pay him the money he owed him. McGlynn had his gun in the right pocket of his gray zipper-down sweatshirt and he pointed it straight at Vinny. Vinny reached into his pockets, taking out all of the money he had just won and placing it on the ground in front of McGlynn. Vinny was crying, begging and pleading for his life, with his hands crossed looking up at the most cold-hearted guy in New York.

Vinny begged him, "Please Fuzzy, I swear I'll get you the rest of the money, I fuckin' swear!"

Bang, Bang, Bang, Bang!

McGlynn fired four shots into Vinny Morelli. Vinny thrashed on the ground for a few seconds before his lips and mouth spewed blood and his convulsions ceased. He lay there, lifeless, and Fuzzy picked up the cash and dashed across the street. He grabbed a bus four blocks away and headed back to Brooklyn. Fuzzy knew that six grand out of this guy was a fuckin' gift and that it would probably never come his way again. He decided to cut his losses and move on. Vinny Morelli was dead at the age of fifty-four.

Eddie's fourth grade teachers were shocked at how smart this kid was. He was entered in the math bee and ended up representing his grade in the New York State Math Competition, which took place later that year in Syracuse. He came in second at that event, losing to an eighth grader from Our Lady of Victory on Long Island.

His basketball ability was now starting to get the attention of everyone in the neighborhood. Even at this young age, people knew who he was. He stood at about five-six and was built like a truck. The kids in the park and the schoolyard wanted him on their team and he spent the entire fourth grade kicking their asses. He played on a few different teams that year. He played for the school team at St. Francis, as well as the local team known as the Marine Park Indians. He even played on a few travel teams.

Most of the older kids in the neighborhood would attend basketball camp each summer and Eddie couldn't wait to go. He wasn't old enough yet, but Joe promised him that he could go when he got to the eighth grade, as long as he kept his grades up and paid for a portion of camp himself. Joe always made sure that his kids worked hard if they really wanted something badly enough. He wanted to make sure that his children tried to stay ahead in life and the methods he used so far had been working well for Kathy and him.

That December, Eddie's team played in a CYO Christmas Tournament at St. Rose Elementary School, in Rockaway. His father told all of the kids on the team that Rockaway produced the best basketball talent, and if they thought that Marine Park produced good players, wait until they saw these kids. He warned them that the Rockaway kids could flat out play, and there would be kids from all areas of Brooklyn there, too. Most of Eddie's friends kind of smirked, not really believing that anyone could be as good as they were. They had all been playing together since the first grade when they started with the Indians team, and nobody had ever really put a scare into them yet.

St. Francis got pounded in the first game of the single elimination tournament and started to dress to go home. In a nice way, Joe gave the kids his "I told you so," speech in the locker room right after the game.

"Okay guys, we gave it our best shot," said Joe. "Maybe next year we'll take the teams we haven't seen before a little more seriously, what do ya say?"

Joe made his point. These kids had really gotten a little cocky. Seeking an entry into this tournament was all part of Joe's plan to wake them all up a little bit. It looked as if it had worked.

They were all outside in a caravan of coaches and parents, ready to head home. Eddie had to go to the bathroom so he ran back inside the gym. Eddie trotted past the court where he and his teammates just got pulverized, and heard the squeak of sneakers on the planks of the court's floor and the sound of the referee's whistle. He paused to get a look at the game going on when he saw a kid, about his age, double pump, score a lay-up, get fouled and then step up to the line. *Swish.*

Eddie got back into the car, and as they were half-way home on Beach Channel Drive, he said to his father, "Dad, you should have seen this lefty from a school named St. Leo's. Wow, could he play."

FRANKIE WAS ZIPPING THROUGH THE fourth grade with ease. He just won the school math bee for the fourth grade, and he took second in the fourth and fifth grade spelling bee. He was sitting in class during a half day of school just waiting for Easter to arrive. His CYO basketball team just won the Brooklyn/ Queens Championship over the weekend and he was bragging to the rest of the class about his 17 points, 11 rebounds, and 12 assists. He was sitting at his desk before his class started, talking to a bunch of his friends. They all made sure to listen very attentively when he spoke, and if they didn't, he'd tell them to fuckin' pay attention.

"Those Bayside kids in the first game were good. The Forest Hills kids sucked!" said Frankie, as he spoke of this past weekend's opponent. "That one little dick, number fourteen, he kept fuckin' grabbin' my arm under the basket."

Some of his listeners had actually never heard these words before and they were dying to hear more. They were all gathered around Frankie while he was talking. Their eyes were widening as he was letting out one curse after another.

"I spit on my hand before I shook that asshole's hand after the game," said Frankie, sneering in a jocular way while he was telling the rest of the kids.

The other kids were laughing, in part, because they liked Frankie's stories, but more because Frankie made them nervous enough to be a little giddy. They were falling out of their seats, laughing their asses off. They thought Frankie was the greatest. This guy would say anything.

That day's class lesson was one of those pre-holiday lessons that you get when you're in grammar school. You know the ones, the Wednesday before Thanksgiving, the day before Christmas Eve, or the Wednesday before Holy Thursday. Being that St. Leo's was a Catholic school, those days were always half days and there was either a party or some bullshit game just to keep the kids occupied until the 11:30 dismissal. Most teachers would wrap these days up at 11:15 anyway, anticipating a few days free of all of these pain-in-the-ass kids. Frankie was the biggest pain-in-the-ass of all. Most of the teachers actually liked him, but none of them wanted him in their class.

That year, he had been placed in the hands of Mrs. Dana Mongello. Mrs. Mongello was a ten-year veteran who was very well-respected among her peers and all of the students in the school. All of the boys in the school were in love with her. She was tall, with dark hair, and had a great set of legs. She was a graduate of the University of North Carolina and received her masters in education at Brooklyn College. She could have made much more money in a public school, but she was a local girl from a big Dyker Heights family with money, so this place was home to her. She was tough, yet fair; funny, yet she knew when to draw the line. She was actually the perfect teacher for Frankie.

One way that Mrs. Mongello liked to fill some time was to ask the kids to talk about their favorite movies. This erased at least an hour from the meaningless day and it was something most of these fourth graders enjoyed, so Mrs. Mongello was thrilled. The whole idea was to go around the room and ask each kid to say what their favorite movie was and then give a brief description of what they perceived it to be about. Most kids picked the one that was most fresh in their mind and no one dared to pick anything that would have graphic descriptions. Every kid said pretty much the same thing — *Major League, Look Who's Talking, Indiana Jones.*

When they got to Frankie, he stood up and was just about to say his movie. Before he started to speak, you could see the look in Mrs. Mongello's eyes. She had a bunch of things going through her mind at that moment. *Please, say anything, Fletch Lives, Field Of Dreams, anything for Christ's sake!* Her thought ended and he came out with it. Frankie put his foot on the seat of his desk, leaned his right elbow down on his knee, looked around the room at his peers and he shouted out *"Let It Ride!"* Mrs. Mongello, having never heard of the film, actually breathed a sigh of relief and muttered under her breath, "Wow, I'm impressed, the mere sound of it is innocent enough." She said aloud, "Okay Frankie, tell us what that's about," praying like hell it was about two kids on a roller coaster or something.

"Well Mrs. M, I saw *Back to the Future* a few years ago, and it has always been my favorite movie until now. *Let It Ride* is about a degenerate gambler named Jay Trotter who couldn't get a break, until his stupid friend, Looney, ended up giving him the tip of his life and he hit race after race at the track. Turned out to be the best day of his life."

Frankie smiled and sat down. There really wasn't much of a reaction from his classmates for a few reasons. First of all, they were nine. Secondly, they had probably never even heard of a horse tip, much less, a guy having the best day of his life betting on one. They did clap however, but that's because they were all scared shit of this kid.

You really couldn't tell what stunned Mrs. Mongello more. The word "degenerate" coming out of the mouth of a fourth grader or the fact that a movie about a horse player interested him enough to tell the class about it, smiling ear to ear. She had seen the news and read the articles about what happened to Frankie's dad two years back. In a way, she probably thought that this was the way that Frankie wished it had been for his dad. She was probably just happy he didn't say *Best fuckin' day of his life*, two days prior to Good Friday in a Catholic school.

She just smiled and said, "Nice job, Frankie."

Frankie smiled back at Mrs. Mongello, like he and she now knew each other more intimately. He sat down, wished every-one in the class a Happy Easter, and waited to be dismissed.

Eddie had just graduated from the eighth grade and was getting ready for high school. He spent his first official day of his summer at Rockaway Beach with a few of his friends. They had a great day and looked forward to a summer full of beach and basketball. When he got home that night his dad sat him down out on the small deck in the back of their house and told him that a guy that he works with had his son working as a caddy in a town called Garden City on Long Island.

Joe said, "You know that kid Troop Snyder on your summer league team?"

"Yeah," said Eddie.

"Do you know what he does every morning in the summer?"

"No, what?" asked Eddie.

"He gets his ass up out of bed and goes all the way out to

Long Island on the train to caddy for the golfers at The Garden Oaks Country Club. Do you know how much money he made there last summer?"

"How much?"

"Five thousand dollars," said Joe, with a huge smile across his face.

Eddie didn't look interested at all. He was bouncing a basketball on the wooden deck, not paying a bit of attention to what his dad said.

Joe wasn't a huge drinker, but he enjoyed a few cold beers in the summer. He was sitting there, staring at this clueless kid of his. He reached his hand down into his small igloo cooler, cracked open a Coors Light, and said, "Let me ask you a question, Eddie."

"Sure, Dad."

"Did you have fun at the beach today?"

"Yeah, why?"

"Because it was your last day there, that's why. I am driving you out to Long Island tomorrow. You're going caddying. You can take the train home with Troop, he's a year older than you so mom and I won't be as nervous. Then you can start taking the train in with him in the mornings."

"But what about basket......."

Joe cut him off. "You'll still be able to play in the Rockaway League, and carrying golf bags will keep you in great shape for the season. Also, you have no idea what kind of connections you can make at a place like that. People who belong to clubs are people with money, who offer kids jobs when they get older. It happens all the time, believe me."

"Dad, come on. I already have a job lined up over at the horse stable this summer, walking horses. A kid on my team does it, and he makes good money." He was starting to cry a bit. "Please Dad, I don't want to go all the way to Long Island, please!"

"You're going. You'll see Troop tonight at your summer league game, and you can ask him how you should dress. I am waking you up at five am."

Eddie wasn't really crazy about this idea at all. He wanted to enjoy his summer. He had his heart set on walking the horses at the stables in Rockaway. Their jobs started each morning at about 5:00, but they were done by 10:00. He knew he'd have plenty of beach-time, and time to play basketball.

Anyone who has ever been a caddy knows that the caddy yard is a place that every kid should experience. People wouldn't think it, but being a caddy creates tough skin, and makes you see people for who they really are. When a kid grows up caddying, or "looping," as it's called, they learn more about life than any fuckin' part-time job bagging groceries, that's for sure. They also meet some of the funniest fuckin' people in the entire world.

As a caddy, a kid will meet some of the biggest assholes who think who they are just because they've made a few bucks in life and they got some little piss-on carrying their forty-five pound bag all over the goddamn golf course. They generally pack their golf bag with ten-dozen balls, keep their irons in individual tubes with covers on the iron heads and carry two umbrellas and a fuckin' ball retriever. They are usually the ones who help themselves to the orange water coolers first, while the caddies are standing right next to them with their swollen shoulders and parched throats.

A kid will also meet other guys who they admire so much because they have made those same few bucks, but have never forgotten where they came from. These are the golfers who earn your respect because they treat you with it, and they tip you accordingly. They address caddies by their first names, ask them where they go to school, and always make sure they take extra clubs with them towards their shots, in order to save the looper a few steps. These are what caddies call, "The best loops in the club." Everybody wants to loop for these guys.

Starting out as a caddy requires a whole lot of patience. Some guys would never be able to last. They quit after a day, two days tops. This shit happened all the time. Eddie was about to find out that sometimes in life, patience pays off, and wow, was he going to have to learn how to be patient.

On his first day down at the caddy yard, he walked in and saw about thirty kids sitting on benches. The ones on the benches were very quiet, and they were usually the kids who were new on the scene. They were shittin' in their pants and they were absolutely starving. Most new kids had no idea if they were permitted to bring breakfast or not. They would sit there watching the older kids sinking their teeth into their ham and cheese omelets with fuckin' cheese oozing out; talking about how many cheap Keystone Light beers they shot-gunned the night before, and how lucky they were to have made it home alive. One group in the yard even referred to themselves as the fuckin' "Keystone Posse." There was never a sober day at the yard for that crew.

The new kids had been sitting there since 6:00 waiting for a loop, all of them trying to beat the other new kids to the yard, trying to show the boss that they were there first. They would run to the parking lot, hustling bags from the trunks of the golfers who pulled up, and walk as close as they could to the caddy master so he would notice what they were doing, hoping this would be just enough ass-kissing to get a loop. Occasionally, there would be a kid who would run a bag in, holding it on his shoulder completely backwards. At most jobs, co-workers would just run over and help the new guy out, telling him to turn the bag around. Not at the caddy yard though. This job was so competitive. Kids would just fuckin' crack up laughing, telling the rookie that the way he was holding the bag was perfect, hoping he would continue to hold it that way for the rest of the summer.

After Eddie found his seat on one of the benches he began to look around and wonder how the fuck this all works down here. He looked out to a giant light blue desk with wheels on it. Behind the desk sat the caddy master, Freddie, the meanest guy Eddie had ever laid eyes on in his life. This guy was about seventy years old. He smoked about a carton of Kool cigarettes a day, and sucked down green Vicks cough drops like they were fuckin' skittles. He loved the power that he had over the kids. He had a tight head of Brillo hair and a big nose. He used to point to the golf bags with his crooked fingers as he called each kid's name for their loop. He was a hard worker though, and if a kid ever tried to leave early because they got sick of waiting around, or split, when he needed them to make a second loop late in the day, look the fuck out!

There was kind of a tradition at this particular yard that had been going on, probably since Ben Hogan was a fuckin' looper. If a kid didn't get a loop by about 11:00 in the morning, and it was looking like they'd miss out on an entire day of summer, they would leap out the back window of the caddy shack in the back of the yard. The shack smelled like a fuckin' Porta Potty, so most of the kids would just hold their breath as they made their escape. They'd walk home on the tracks of the Long

Island Railroad acting like they were bad-asses because they were walking five feet from the third rail, and thinking they had put one over on Freddie. Little did they know, although Freddie may have been old, he knew everything that went on down there. He used to keep a list of all the kids who cut out. He kept his looper inventory right down to the fuckin' cheap-ass, Puma knock-off, Mark V sneakers the kid was wearing before the exit. He always got revenge on a caddy who left him hanging.

One time, this kid, Kehrli O'Hanlon, a little shrimp with bright blonde hair, wanted to leave early to go to his local town pool with his friends. O'Hanlon had already been busted for jumping out the back window the summer before so he decided to try some new bullshit on the old man. This idiot thought it would be a good idea to tell Freddie the caddy master that he had Yankee tickets with his dad. The next day he sat there all day long, watching some kids make two loops before he got one. When he went up and asked Freddie why he had not gotten out all day, the old man looked at him and said "Check the fuckin' schedule next time you stupid little mutha fucka, the fuckin' Yankees were in Chicago yesterday, what did you and your father take the fuckin' Concord out there? Take a one week W.O.P. to think about it."

A W.O.P. down at the yard simply stood for WITHOUT PAY. The old bastard would make kids stay home for a week and give them the heaviest fuckin' bags in the club when they returned after their week of punishment. The guys with the heavy bags were usually the shittiest loops in the tri-state area. W.O.P.'s were the worst, but they turned boys into men. Freddie was actually the only form of structure in some kids' lives. He was nuts, but he served a good purpose.

Freddie would sit there calling names of kids, as each member would make his way out to the first tee. Eddie was so confused as to how the hell some of these older kids were just walking in at 8:30 or 9:00, not having waited a minute on these old broken-down benches, grabbing their bags of choice, and heading right up the 1st fairway. This was Eddie's first taste of seniority.

Eddie sat on that bench for four straight days. He would go there each day at 6:00 am and stay until 3:00 pm with nothin' but a bunch of fuckin' splinters in his ass, and a *caddy insurance* policy that he purchased from this wise ass named Jack Eschmann, from Stewart Manor, a small town on the Garden City border. Jack was a sharp-looking kid. He had a smirk on him, that when you first met him, you might wanna kick his ass, but after knowing him a while, people got to like him because he was a real fuckin' character. There was obviously no such thing as *caddy insurance*, but this was one of those scams this guy Jack would pull, just to try to bust a few kids' balls and get a few laughs. If he liked you, and you played along with his joke, without being a fuckin' baby about it, most times he'd give you your money back.

Eddie played along with Jack's antics, but he was really starting to get disappointed. No beach with his friends, no hoops at the park all day, and no fuckin' loop. He begged his father each night to let him take that job walking the ponies, but his dad kept telling him to hang in there. He was just about to give up for good one Friday morning, when fate stepped in.

One of the older caddies named Sully walked over to him as he was sitting there on the bench, doing nothing, but trying to spit on the ground in the exact same spot where he hocked his previous loogie. He sat down next to Eddie and started to talk to him. This was the first kid who said a word to him all week, besides Troop Snyder and Jack Eschmann.

"What's your name, kid?" asked Sully. Sully was about five-nine, with brown hair and an Irish-looking face. He was a riot. He would basically say anything to anyone. He didn't give a shit. He was feared by every caddy and loved by every member. Most of the members were intimidated by him because he was a much better golfer than they were. He'd snicker as he was looping, every time a guy fucked up a shot, even wising off to a few guys, in jest of course, telling them to take up tennis. The loopers were scared of him because he was a black belt in Karate. Every now and then, just to spook a new kid, he would stand in front of them in the fuckin' Mr. Miyagi canoe pose. He had a hot temper too. He drove a black Nova that could only go in drive, the reverse gear was shot. The previous summer, he was going to the Bruce Springsteen concert at Jones beach with his two friends, Gucky Jackson and Yogi Ferrick; and Yogi forgot the tickets. Sully was so pissed off at Yogi, he shifted from drive to reverse at about seventy-five miles an hour. The car never went in reverse again. Sometimes, while making a "deli run," he'd make a few of the new caddies push his car backwards out of his parking spot as he was sitting behind the wheel, laughing at them, the whole time.

"What are you fuckin' deaf? I said what's your name?"

"I'm Eddie."

"Eddie, I'm Sully."

Eddie had no idea if this guy was gonna kick the shit out of him or shake his hand, and he was shittin' in his pants.

"What's your last name, Eddie?"

"Mullaney."

"Where you from?" asked Sully.

"Brooklyn, it's not around here," offered Eddie.

"What do you think, I don't know where the fuck Brooklyn is," snapped Sully. "What the fuck are you doing all the way out here?"

"It's a long story. My dad made me come down."

Sully paused for a second or two. He was eying Eddie up and down as he did with just about every new kid who entered the yard. Sully was a huge basketball fan and he knew that this kid had to have played ball, he was so fuckin' tall, and he just looked liked a ball player. Eddie just sat there in silence. He was staring straight ahead at the first tee. All he could think about was how badly he wanted to get the fuck out of that caddy yard. He hated being the new guy. He stood out more than any of the new kids and he was fed up with just sitting there every single day for nothing. Sully was now sitting right next to him, eating his ham, egg and cheese, drinking his Quik chocolate milk, and burping loud enough that the guys who were teeing off could hear him. Eddie was still staring straight ahead with a half a smile on him that didn't even look close to real, and a face that was bright red, full of nerves and embarrassment, having no idea what the hell this Sully guy was gonna do next.

Sully got up off the bench, crumpled up the aluminum foil from his sandwich and shot it into the garbage can on the opposite side of the yard like he was shooting a jump shot. He headed right out to the caddy master and said, "Freddie, I want that tall skinny red-headed kid out with me today." Sully practically ran the fuckin' place so Freddie, in turn, did as he said.

Eddie got his first loop two minutes later with Sully and

was about to enter the real world very quickly. Sully had balls the size of melons. One day, he saw a guy cheat by kicking his own ball in the rough. Imagine that, cheating at a gentlemen's sport. Sully walked over and said, "Hey, I saw that. Just make sure there's a fuckin' Ben Franklin in my hand at the end of the round and we'll let it slide." The member was in shock as Sully winked at him and walked back onto the fairway lugging his two bags on his shoulders. He was the best, and he got that Ben Franklin too.

The rule at the halfway house was that caddies were permitted one soda. Sully would totally ignore that rule and just order two of everything. He would say to Efram, the Spanish guy behind the counter, "Hey, you fuckin' hump, gimme a tuna and cheese sandwich, two ice teas, and two Almond Joys, and give skinny here whatever the fuck he wants too. Make sure you put it on his bill," pointing to the member he had just caught cheating, still smiling at the member, and scratching the bridge of his nose with his middle finger.

When Eddie's first loop ended, he walked away with fifty bucks, a huge smile, and a ton of new knowledge from Sully. "Hey Junior," said Sully, as he was tucking his crisp hundred-dollar bill in his wallet. "Don't take shit from anybody, especially the shit loops." The members were literally ten feet from him.

Eddie was so glad that he had finally made a friend, the most senior guy there, to boot. His caddy career had begun, and he split his funds between his three wallets in his room, just as he always did.

JUNE 17, 1994. FRANKIE JUST finished eighth grade gradu-ation practice at around 2:00 pm and was heading home to get ready for an evening wedding. He was an usher in his uncle's wedding and he had to get into his tux. Frankie's father had two brothers from Long Island, and although Frankie didn't see them all that much, he loved his uncles and always had a good time with them the few times a year that he saw them. Both of his uncles loved to gamble, which was no real surprise after knowing his father. They didn't bet as often as Vinny, but they definitely loved action and big sporting events. They hadn't missed a trip to the Final Four or the Super Bowl since they were nineteen-years-old, and the day that they were about to have was so full of action it would go down, according to them, as the best wedding for any gambler in the history of weddings. Frankie would be there too, and not only would he witness it all, but he'd fall in love with the action as well.

Frankie's Uncle Louie beeped the horn as he pulled up next to him in his black 1986 IROC-Z. Frankie waited for him after graduation practice but he never showed up. Louie was apologizing up and down for being late but he got stuck in the city at the Ranger parade. The New York Rangers just won the Stanley Cup for the first time since 1940, and he couldn't help but celebrate a bit. Louie, better known as "Lucky Louie the Clammer," was a local bartender on the weekends and full-time clam digger out on the far end of Long Island during the week. Louie had originally planned to take the train into the parade but the Long Island Railroad was on strike, so he was forced to drive in. No train strike was gonna stop him from seeing that parade.

As uncle Louie's car came to a full stop he had the fuckin' *Jerky Boys* tape crankin' on his radio. He was both half-bombed and half-dressed, sporting tuxedo pants and a blue Ranger jersey. Louie was a former college hockey star with long brown hair and a scar on his chin from an out-of-control check that he put on one of his opponents a few years back. He stunk of Grand Marnier and Budweiser. His Marlboro cigarette was hanging out of his mouth with the ash of the cigarette butt almost hitting the steering wheel, and there were still some small pieces of parade ticker tape stuck in his hair. This guy was primed for the wedding. He had the *New York Post* on his lap as he was driving, checking the line on the Knick game that night.

The Knicks were playing the Rockets that night in Game 5 of the NBA finals, and they were two-point favorites. Louie had a small TV packed in the back seat of his car that he was going to ask the catering hall to hook up, just in case they didn't have a TV. Most brides and grooms would take offense at the concept of a guest bringing a television, but not this particular pair. Surprisingly, the bride-to-be actually suggested it.

Frankie's other uncle was about to hit the jackpot with this bride. Uncle Fee was about to marry a hot blonde from Levittown named Sugar. She was tall, she had a beautiful face with fine details, long legs and arms that gave her a height of five-ten, and she could dance better than Madonna herself. Rumor had it, that for her introduction song at the reception, Sugar actually asked the DJ to play the song that the racetrack plays when the horses come onto the track, knowing that would be a great surprise for her new husband.

Frankie and Louie met up with Fee in the back of Our Lady of Lourdes Church before the ceremony. Fee was sharply dressed. He stood about six-three with his black hair slicked back, a small mustache, and a pack of True Blue's in the breast pocket of his tuxedo. He wore a white tux jacket with tails, black pants, and a black pair of patent leather tux shoes. Fee had just handed the altar boys, Robert and Randy, a hundred bucks each for serving the mass and told them to "Make it nice for Sugar." They were so shocked with the tip, they were smiling during the mass as much as the guests were. Fee never believed in tipping, it was over-tipping that he considered an absolute *must* in life.

Fee Morelli was a crazy fuckin' New York City fireman and nobody ever messed with him. He used to bang his head on a wall before he went into a fire to pump up the rest of the truck, just like that fuckin' lunatic "Firemen Ed" does at the Jet games. Fee was excited to be getting married and he looked over at the priest, Fr. Wagner, as they were all getting ready in the back of the church, and said, "Hey Padre, make this quick, we got pictures to take and the Knicks start in an hour and a half."

Father Wagner had no idea what the hell this guy was talking about, but he gave a sermon that lasted all of three minutes. Fee was glaring at the priest to move along quickly, holding Sugar close to him after they took their vows, and looking up at the Church ceiling. He was winking up at his brother Vinny, and his younger cousin Richie, who had just passed a few weeks before the wedding, feeling sorry they couldn't be with him and Sugar, but knowing that they were watching.

They were all reception-bound and ready to go. Frankie smoked his first joint that night, sharing a "Jeff Spicoli size" joint with a guy named Jerry. Jerry was a big guy, about 350 pounds with a red face and stringy brown hair. He told Frankie that if he didn't take a hit of the joint that he'd kick the shit out of him.

The guests had arrived at GiGi's in Westbury. The crowd of three hundred people were piling in, and the bridal party had a nice buzz going. It was looking like a good night all around. Uncle Louie and his pal, Jimmy Morrisey, were standing by the bar in the cocktail area as Louie was getting ready to line up with the rest of the enormous bridal party for their introductions. Louie was smokin' a butt and singing the words to Billy Joel's *Scenes From An Italian Restaurant*. Morrisey was going on about the recent Stanley Cup Championship. He and Louie were recapping the exciting seven game series and talking about the victory parade in the City that day. They were both drinking cold Buds and toasting the Rangers.

Morrisey was one of about a dozen Irish guys in Fee's firehouse. He was a little guy with brown hair who wore an old Ranger T-shirt under his gear every time he fought a fire.

"Finally, man," said Louie, yelling to Morrisey above

the music. "Remember all of those disappointing seasons, man?"

"I sure do," said Morrisey. "Some fuckin' Islander fan in my firehouse came in the day after the Rangers season was over last year, wearing a goddamn Potvin jersey just to rub it in. Fuckin' 'probie' tryin' to make a joke. The kid made a big mistake, Lou."

Louie laughed. "No way, what'd ya do?"

Morrisey smirked. "Well, since it was my turn to cook that night, I thought about puttin' a little Exlax in his chicken parm, but I settled on punchin' him in the fuckin' mouth instead. He never wore that jersey again, I can tell ya that much."

Louie was cracking up laughing at Morrisey's story, holding his hand by his nose to try and stop the beer from shooting out of it. After he calmed down, he was starting to wonder what the hell happened to Frankie. He hadn't seen him for a while. Frankie came running into the room and headed straight for Louie.

"Uncle Louie, you're not gonna fuckin' believe this!" said Frankie.

Louie was looking at the kid like he was nuts. "Believe what?" asked Louie, with a cloud of his own cigarette smoke in front of him.

"OJ Simpson's fuckin' dead!" exclaimed Frankie.

Louie had a bewildered look about him like Frankie had to have been out of his fuckin' mind. He straightened his bow tie with his left hand, held the bottle of Bud in his right and took a sip of his beer.

Morrisey chimed in. "What do you mean he's dead, he's not dead, I heard he just got arrested, what are you fuckin' stoned, Frankie?"

Frankie responded, "Yes, actually, I am stoned, thanks to that big guy over there," said Frankie, pointing to Jerry. "But I heard that OJ shot himself in the back of his own truck!"

"No way!" said Louie. "Are you sure?"

"I'm positive, Uncle Louie, the valet parkers are listening to the news on the radio." Frankie's pupils were completely dilated but he looked like he was making sense.

When they were heading into the reception there was already a buzz all around about OJ. People were saying that the cops were chasing him on a freeway in California and that he pulled over and did himself in. There wasn't a TV in sight, and these guys were dying to know what the fuck happened. Turned out, there was OJ action going on, but he wasn't dead. He was being chased down the freeway in a white Bronco.

The dance floor was packed with people right away, dancing to the tunes of DJ Paul McGuire. The catering hall was trying to get the best man's speech going so they could get ready to serve the food, but this crowd just refused to stop dancing, and Fee kept telling the DJ, "One more song, we got plenty of time to eat." This was the best wedding crowd GiGi's had ever seen. Frankie had never been to a wedding before, so he didn't know what to expect. At first, he acted like he was way too fuckin' cool to be dancing. That didn't last for too long. Before you knew it, Frankie was wearing dark sunglasses, playing the air guitar, and singing The Archies song, "Sugar Sugar" to his new aunt, Sugar Morelli. The Sister Sledge Song "We Are Family" was re-written that night when Sugar and the girls grabbed the mic and started singing to the groom, "We are family, I got all my sisters and Fee!"

After the guests sat down to eat, and Fee's two friends, Marty and Erik, gave their best man speeches, there was a huge crowd outside of the manager's office. Fee had sixteen ushers in his bridal party and every single one of them was gathered outside of the office watching the only television in the building, courtesy of Louie Morelli. He ran out to the car to grab his TV that he packed for the Knick game, and luckily, there was a cable hook up in the building. The best part was that Sugar, and Fee's sister, Diane, would even stop by from time to time to find out the Knicks score and see if the guys needed a fresh beer. The Knicks were up 48-37 at the half, the series was tied 2-2, and every single one of Fee's boys thanked Louie about five times each, for bringing that fuckin' television.

"Can you believe this shit?" asked Louie. These guys loved the action, and Frankie thought that this was the greatest thing in the world. Guys were calling their bookies trying to bet the second half of the Knicks-Rockets game when, all of a sudden, Lucky Louie started taking action on OJ Simpson. These guys were literally making bets on whether this guy was going to live or fuckin' shoot himself.

They had gone back and forth for a while, Knicks, OJ, Knicks, OJ. They were finally starting to get heavily into the Knick game and didn't even have the option of going back and forth anymore. NBC had cut the Knick game off to show this idiot being driven down the freeway with his buddy, Al Cowlings, behind the wheel of his truck. When they cut the game off, guys were going nuts! One guy, Alan, grabbed the manager and told him to turn the fuckin' game back on or he would stab him with a butter knife. The little manager, who looked like Tattoo from *Fantasy Island*, pleaded with Alan to let him go. He started to scream, "Please let me go, let me go, it's not me, NBC did it!"

The reception ended with the microphone in Sugar Morelli's hand, singing an old disco song to her new husband. The song was called "Heaven Must Be Missing An Angel." Heaven was missing one for sure. This girl had her wedding interrupted by her new husband and his pals betting on both a Knick game and a former football star turned fugitive, and she never stopped smiling. They all had a great time that Friday night in June of '94.

Fee was getting ready to address the crowd and toast his new bride. "Ladies and gents, I just want to thank everyone for coming, and I hope you had a good time tonight. Sugar, you look so beautiful, I love you baby." The guy looked like a star. He was standing there with the DJ's wireless microphone in one hand, and his cocktail in the other.

There was one particular table paying very close attention in the back of the room. All of Fee's ushers were at that table, looking right at Fee, knowing this wasn't going to be the usual wedding reception speech. They knew this guy had some information about their bets.

Their table had cigarette butts piled a foot high in their ashtrays. There were fifty or sixty empty Bud bottles lined up on the table, that when viewed from above, spelled out OJ. They were waiting for the scoop. There was $760 piled up on the table. Frankie was the only one who said that OJ would be arrested before 1:00 am Eastern. Everyone else was out already, saying he was going to pull the fuckin' trigger. Louie had put the money up for Frankie so he could be a part of the action.

Fee continued, "One more thing, the Knicks..." Everyone was on the edge of their seats, these guys all bet the Knicks and had more on the fuckin' game than they had stuffed in the envelopes.

Fee screamed, "They won 91-84, they covered baby!" The

place went wild. These guys made a fortune. "One last thing," Fee said. Frankie was drunk, stoned, with his eyes glued to Uncle Fee, his new hero. "Congrats Frankie, they just locked up OJ. The son-of-a-bitch is still alive!"

The ushers lifted Frankie up like they were taking "Rudy" off the fuckin' football field. The place was going crazy. Frankie had just won $760 on the OJ chase. Frankie's empire was about to begin and he didn't even know it.

EAST COAST INVITATIONAL BASKETBALL CAMP was held at Manhattan College, in Riverdale, New York. Most of the kids who were invited to the camp were the best of the best in New York, New Jersey, and Connecticut for their age group.

Eddie was fully qualified to attend this camp three years ago but he wasn't old enough. When he showed up on the first day, the place was packed. Registration took place in a huge gymnasium at the far end of the camp. Basketball camp is different than most camps. It's not like a regular summer camp where the kids go fishing and play shuffleboard and shit, and it's certainly not like football camp, which is like being in fuckin' prison with shoulder pads on. It was a place where kids played competitive basketball, all day, and hung out back at the campus dorms all night and had a great time. They always tried, although the camp staff was very strict, to get away with as much shit as they could.

All of the kids were starting to line up on the gym floor, waiting to be directed to their rooms. Eddie knew about eighty percent of the camp from playing against most of the kids in his off-season travel team circuit throughout the year. He was waving to a few guys, shakin' a few hands with various coaches, parents of players, and different guys he'd faced all year. From his seat, he looked off to his left and he saw a kid on the far end of the gym. The kid was a lefty, and he had hit nine consecutive three pointers, and he wasn't done yet. "Who the hell is this kid, and where the hell have I seen him before?" Eddie asked himself.

There were a few other guys who started to notice him as well. He had now hit sixteen of seventeen three-pointers. He had not one, but three smaller kids under the basket who were getting his rebounds for him.

"Make sure you hit me in the hands with that fuckin' ball!" yelled the kid to the rebounders.

Eddie and two other guys, Rodrick and Floyd, two tall black kids from Eddie's AAU team, were standing together. They could not believe their eyes. The lefty shooter had now hit twenty-one of twenty-three bombs from behind the arc, as he turned to address his new visitors. He was about five-nine with a sleeveless red T-shirt and a light gray pair of baggy shorts.

"What the fuck are you guys lookin' at?"

Eddie, Rodrick, and Floyd were very surprised by the way they were being spoken to, and they were scared shit of the kid immediately. Eddie did the talking for the three of them.

"Nah, nothin' man. We were just checkin' out your shot," said Eddie.

"Oh yeah? Well I look forward to kickin' your fuckin' ass all week. Now, if you three are gonna keep standin' there, then help these kids grab my fuckin' rebounds," said the kid, as he hit his twenty-seventh three-pointer.

Eddie and the other kids just turned around and walked back to their spots on the other side of the gym while the lefty just kept shooting.

The first night at camp was like a mini draft. All of the courts were packed with kids who had all been split up by age and or skill level. Eddie had lit up most of his opponents until the final game of the night. He went up against that arrogant lefty that he'd met earlier. Eddie stood at about five-ten having sprouted during the summer, and the other kid was more or less the same height.

The two of them had gone back and forth through the whole scrimmage game. They had people coming over to watch the match-up. They were both great players and neither one really gave into the other. There was no score kept on draft night but if one were keeping a book, they'd be writing in about thirty points for each of these guys. They were clearly the "cream of the crop" at the camp. Eddie was always the best player, no matter what group he played with. This was the first time he had ever been challenged and he was enjoying the competition. After the game ended, the kids shook hands and headed back to their rooms to get ready for dinner.

On the way back, Eddie noticed two huge kids had grabbed the sharp-shootin' lefty. This kid wised off to just about everyone in the camp that day, and a couple of soon-to-be eleventh graders from the Bronx were just letting him know that his wise cracks were gonna be on hold for the rest of the week.

There was one guy, Casey Pagnotta, holding the lefty's arms

back in a fuckin' full nelson, while the other one was kicking and punching the kid with everything he had. Pagnotta, more commonly known as "Pags," was a tough kid with slicked back jet-black hair and a five o'clock shadow on his face that he had since the fifth grade. The southpaw was trying his best to get out of the neck hold but he couldn't get free. Pags was too strong. Most kids just walked up and watched, some cheered.

Max Stroehlein, better known as "Stro," was the biggest kid in the camp, and he was pummeling this kid, nailing the lefty in the face with one blow after another. Stro was about six-six and about 195 pounds without a bit of fuckin' fat on him. He wore a tight haircut, and had a raspy, intimidating voice.

Eddie, who had never thrown a punch in his life, came whizzing through the crowd of onlookers and headed right for Stro. He drilled Stro in the face, turning and doing the same thing to Pags. He knew both Stro and Pags, and they both looked kind of confused.

"What the fuck are you doin' Mullaney?" screamed Stro.

"I'm stopping a two-on-one fight, douche bag." Eddie's voice was cracking like he was gonna cry. He had just leveled these two guys and he was the one almost in tears. Eddie really had never fought before, so he didn't know what to do. "Go get dressed assholes, I just did you a favor. If the counselors found out, you'd both be fuckin' going home."

The crowd dispersed and headed back to their rooms. Eddie reached down and helped the kid off of the ground.

The kid whose ass he just saved was wiping the blood off of his mouth as Eddie was helping him up. He addressed Eddie. "Thanks a lot, man. What's your name?"

"Eddie."

"Listen, Eddie, I owe ya one bro. I got a pair of Jordans back in my room that fell off a truck. They're about your size. I'm givin' them to you."

"It's cool man, I don't need your sneakers, but thanks anyway," said Eddie.

"Fuck that! Nobody helps out Frankie Morelli without getting a fuckin' reward. Plus I'll be kickin' your ass all over the court this week anyway, so it's the least I could fuckin' do."

"Eddie smiled, and said "Okay man, thanks a lot, and by the way, what truck did they fall off?"

Frankie just laughed to himself as they walked away, knowing full well that this guy definitely didn't grow up anywhere near his end of Brooklyn. The "fell off a truck" thing was way over his head.

"Listen, Eddie. I'm sorry that I spoke to you like that before. Sometimes I try to be tough and end up lookin' like an asshole."

"No problem, man. I think I saw you at a tournament in Rockaway once. You were pretty good then, and after the way you shot today, I thought I'd save your ass so I could beat the shit out of you this week."

Frankie cracked up laughing and he and Eddie became friends right away, despite their completely different personalities. Ironically, they were headed to the same high school, too.

Frankie and Eddie were stars on the court by day, and cheating card sharks by night. They were scamming everyone at camp. Eddie really had no idea how to play cards when he first met Frankie, but by Wednesday of that week, the kid could have gotten a job as a dealer in Vegas. Frankie was loving it. The guy finally had a smart wing-man. He was a bad influence on Eddie right from the start. These two guys had all kinds of codes, signals and bluffs, and barely even had to use them. They were truly poetry in motion, and nobody could figure it out, not even them.

They didn't stop at cards either. Frankie taught Eddie more shit in six days than a person could learn in a lifetime. Frankie caught on to the "snap-game" from one of the older kids in the neighborhood the summer before. The "snap-game" would drive people fuckin' crazy. Frankie would ask kids to tell him a name of a famous person and somehow he would snap his fingers and say a few things to Eddie, and every single fuckin' time, Eddie would guess exactly who it was. Nobody could ever figure it out. It drove half the camp crazy.

On the last night of camp they had been playing cards with two seniors who thought their shit didn't stink. They stayed up playing until 3:00 am, just the four of them. Frankie and Eddie took two hundred bucks from each of them, and they left their room making fun of these two high school seniors, actually calling them "senior citizens," and laughing all the way down the hall.

Before they had packed up on the last day, Frankie and Eddie split up a total of $815 of their fellow camper's money. Frankie split his share between his sneakers, and Eddie divided his share up between three small wallets that he kept in his bag.

They had gone back and forth all week long at camp, beating the shit out of each other on the court. They shared co-MVP honors on the last day, and looked forward to playing together in high school. Eddie had been upset all summer leading up to camp that he wasn't going to know anyone when he started high school. He was really happy that Frankie was going to the same school.

The Mullaney's showed up on the last day of camp to watch Eddie in the championship and take him home. Frankie was going to take the bus home until Eddie introduced Frankie to his parents and sister. They offered Frankie a ride home, and he accepted, enthusiastically. Frankie spent the whole ride pretending to talk about hoops, but not taking his eyes off of Eddie's little sister, Colleen. He was really diggin' her.

Frankie spent the rest of the summer working at the deli, running the place for his grandfather. He kept the books for him, better than his grandfather could. He used a notebook as his grandfather taught him, but he didn't need to. He tallied money in his head better than a pencil-pushing accountant. One day, there was a situation with the Boar's Head guy named Seamus. He tried to convince Frankie that his grandfather hadn't paid him for a boiled ham. This guy with the meat route was about twenty-five years old with dirty blond hair and pimples. Frankie looked right at the pimply fuck and said, "Oh yeah? You wanna rethink that mutha fucka?"

Seamus took a step forward in Frankie's direction, shocked by the tone of a thirteen-year-old.

"I watched him pay you for the ham last Friday, while you were standing right there," said Frankie, pointing to the red

Good Humor cooler on the opposite side of the deli.

"You took the cash, twenty-nine bucks, if I remember correctly, marked paid on a sheet of white paper and stuffed it in your tan Velcro wallet in the section where you keep your money. You see I was over there, foldin' papers, and you assumed I didn't see what happened. You're trying to put one over on my grandfather because he doesn't speak English so good."

The Boar's Head guy gave him a look and said, "What are you a wiseass? He never fuckin' paid me."

Frankie stood five feet nine inches tall. He had about two inches over Seamus. Frankie turned towards Seamus, squared his shoulders to him, cocked his head and said, "Listen here you fuckin' Irish prick, I saw you do this to him once before, and I never said nothin', probably because I was a lot younger, and wasn't totally sure, but this time I'm sure. Now you got two choices. You can take out your wallet, open it up, and place that white paid receipt on the counter. If you do that, my grandfather will continue to do business with you and we'll try to never have a problem with each other again. The other choice is that you don't take out the fuckin' wallet, and you walk out that door for the last time. It's up to you."

Frankie's grandfather had stopped sweeping the floor in the rear of the store and had made his way to the front. He was staring at his grandson, it was like he had been watching his own boy. The Boar's Head guy backed up a few feet. His shoulders were sloped, and he looked like a deflated balloon. Seamus took out the receipt and placed it on the counter. He shook Frankie's hand and apologized, turned on his heels and walked out.

Vincenzo walked over to Frankie and asked, *"Che*

Sucheso?"

Frankie looked over at his grandfather and said to him in Italian, *"Quel figlio della butana non ci da fastidio piu,"* which, when translated to English, means, *That son-of-a-bitch won't be doing that again.*

Vincenzo, a barrel-chested man, had seen plenty of face-offs in his day. He smiled and finished sweeping the floor, turned and looked at Frankie and said *"Si Fato Buono,"* telling Frankie how proud he was of him. The next morning, right on the curb by Deli of Morelli, there was a brand new meat cooler, courtesy of Seamus and Boar's Head.

Working at the deli wasn't all that Frankie was up to that summer. He was a good-looking kid and he was pretty much the stud of the eighth grade. He'd done what most of the advanced thirteen-year-olds had done, namely made out with a few chicks, and grabbed the baby sitter's ass a few times. Most kids Frankie's age were more concerned with going to the mall, or playing sports in the street, but not Frankie. He was fully focused on trying to lose his virginity before he got to high school. He really had his eyes on Robin, a Jewish girl from Queens, whose father owned the building that the deli occupied. Robin would come around every Friday with her dad. She was about five-five, 110 pounds, with long blond hair and bright blue eyes. She was three years older than Frankie and he was dyin' to bang her. She always assumed that Frankie was older than he was, with all of the responsibilities that he had around the deli. She never asked Frankie his age, so he never told her.

One night, Robin decided to stay in Brooklyn. Her parents were divorced and she was going to spend the night at her mom's house right down the street from the store. That was the night that Frankie got his wish. He banged her three times that night, right in his own bedroom, and he was on top of the world.

The next day, when Frankie was opening up the store, he couldn't stop thinking about the great night he just had with this high school senior. The only problem was he couldn't get his mind off Colleen Mullaney. He was so pissed that when the Mullaney's dropped him off that he forgot to get Eddie's number. He really missed his new friend, too.

Eddie could have easily kept walking that day at camp when Frankie was getting the shit kicked out of him, but he didn't. Eddie hung in there, and slapped around a few kids who he had actually been friends with, and Frankie would never forget it. He was also hoping like hell he'd see Colleen again.

One night, just as the summer was coming to a close, Frankie and Nicky Ventimiglia were out at Frannie Monaco's Bowling Alley, the local hang-out for any of the Bensonhurst kids who were under the age of fifteen. They were playing video games, knockin' back a few *dirty water dogs* and drinking soda. This bowling alley was like something out of the '50s. It only had about eight lanes, old pins, and the smelliest red and tan shoe rentals around. Bowlers always begged to wear their own sneakers when they bowled there. The place had two video games. One of them was an old Pac-Man machine that was completely stained with soda. The other was a Golden Tee Golf machine that was in decent shape. Frankie loved video golf, and he and Nicky would play that machine every chance they got. On this particular night they noticed a couple of kids they had never seen before walk in and start looking around. One guy, whose name was Willie, looked about sixteen. He was wearing a pair of baggy jeans, a long-sleeve white T-shirt, and a sideways Phoenix Suns hat. He had a peach fuzz mustache and a giant gold necklace that made Flavor Flav's clock look like a fuckin' penny on a string. The other guy, Hector, was dressed pretty much the same way. He hung back a few feet, tough but tempered. He wore an oversized pair of outdated Reebok Pumps, baggy shorts, a backwards Celtic's hat, and a T-shirt that read, "Brooklyn's in the House." He looked about seventeen or eighteen-years-old.

They made their way around the bowling alley, giving fist pounds. The place was pretty crowded. Frankie noticed that they had been collecting money from a few guys and handing sheets of paper out to other guys. He and Nicky really couldn't tell what was going on, but they were pretty sure these guys weren't selling fuckin' M&M's. Willie and Hector finished walking around and they started to make their way over to the video machines. When Frankie saw them coming, he pretended that he was glued to his game.

The kids walked over and each put two quarters on top of the golf machine. Hector, the older kid, looked at Frankie and spoke, "Yo man, I got next."

"Next what?" asked Frankie.

"Next fuckin' game, punk!" said Hector.

Frankie pointed to Nicky, who had next game, and responded to Hector, "What the fuck does my buddy look like, a mirage?"

Hector angled his brown eyes on Frankie with a look that could pierce glass. Frankie's entire basketball team was bowling over at lane five, so he really wasn't too scared of these guys, even though he had never seen them before. He knew his team would have his back.

Hector gave Frankie a hefty shove in his shoulder that knocked the back of his head on the video machine. Frankie fell to the ground, holding the back of his head and resting on his knees.

"Your friend looks like a little punk and so do you, mutha fucka," yelled Hector. "Now I got fuckin' next!"

As if on cue, Frankie picked himself up off the ground, cocked his neck back and sent a head butt right at Hector's fuckin' face. The kid's nose broke open like a piñata. Blood spewed all over the video machines, on Frankie's face and on the floor. Frankie was surprised. He figured he'd be in for a little bit more of a fight, but the toes of Hector's sneakers were pointed straight up at the ceiling as he lay on the floor flat on his back. His face was a fuckin' mess, and his white Celtic's hat was lying on the floor of the bowling alley in a puddle of his own blood. Nicky didn't do shit. He really didn't have to. Willie helped Hector off of the ground and dragged him out of the bowling alley, leaving behind the stack of papers they came in with.

Frankie reached down and grabbed a stack of these white sheets that had fanned out on the floor. They listed every single college football game on one side and every pro game on the other. Frankie grabbed a tenth grade on-looker named Richie Beckenburg who would come to the deli on Saturday mornings with his Pop. Richie was the first guy to greet the two kids who just stumbled out, and he had one of the sheets. Frankie pulled Richie aside gently by his shirt, wiped some blood off his own forehead and whispered to him, "What the fuck are these things, Beck?"

Richie was the tallest sixteen-year-old in Brooklyn. He looked like a white version of Manute Bol, standing six feet five inches tall. Richie explained to Frankie that these were weekly parlay sheets. Frankie told Richie to have a seat, and told everyone to go back to lane five. The rest of the kids dispersed and Frankie sat down with Beckenburg. He looked at him and said, "Richie, I wanna know where these came from and how they work."

Richie said, "These things are fuckin' great, Morelli. The more winners you pick, the more you win. If you hit like let's say, four for four, and you bet ten bucks, you win a hundred bucks. Four for four is ten to one odds!"

"Let me ask you a question, Beck." Frankie spoke in a low voice as he leaned into Richie's right ear. "You ever hit four for four on one of these?"

"No. I never have," said Richie.

Frankie smiled at Richie, knowing already what this kid two years older than him hadn't figured out. "That's what I thought," Frankie said. "Do me a favor, Richie. Tell all these fuckin' guys here that if they're looking for a sheet next week, to stop by the deli, any day between six in the morning and nine at night, until school starts. After that, pick-up night will be Tuesdays and collection night will be Thursdays, as soon as school gets out. I'm in charge of these fuckin' sheets from now on."

Richie placed both hands tentatively on Frankie's shoulders. "Frankie, that's nuts, you can't start doing this man. Those two punks work for a guy. If you try to do this on your own and someone hits ten for ten on you, you're fucked!"

But what Richie couldn't know was that Frankie considered himself fully bank-rolled. He had saved money towards his high school tuition. He paid for everything himself, without ever asking anyone for a handout. The only reason he hadn't been running these sheets already was because he didn't know about them. He had five grand in his shoebox, and all he wanted to do now was add to it.

"I'll see you next week, Beck, and by the way, I'll give you two bucks for every kid you bring to me." Frankie patted Richie on the shoulder. "We got a deal?"

Richie nodded his head yes and by the end of the week, he became Brooklyn's tallest sheet runner.

THERE WERE THREE HUNDRED AND fifteen freshmen seated in the St. Elizabeth's auditorium on the first day of school. The boys were wearing freshly pressed but oddly fitting ties and the girls were all sitting with their hands folded on their laps. They were staring attentively at the principal, Brother Stanley, who stood at the podium like a soldier.

Frankie still had not run into Eddie yet, nor had he heard a word of what the principal was saying. He just kept looking around, hoping that the kids would soon be sent to homeroom. He knew that it was likely that he'd find Eddie there since their names were so close alphabetically.

The first day of school was bullshit. Get your locker, run through the schedule, get your textbooks. The school was huge to all of them, and they spent the first few hours just getting accustomed to their new surroundings. All of the kids were scared at the sight of the other three hundred plus kids, except for one kid of course. Frankie just encountered a bunch of new customers, and he was going to capitalize. He had already introduced himself to a few seniors when he was outside waiting for the school doors to open. Some seniors volunteered to assist at freshman orientation and Frankie knew exactly which market to exploit. This kid didn't even get his schedule yet, and he already had sixty bucks in football sheet money on him from a half a dozen upper classman, thirty in the right pocket and thirty in the left.

As Frankie headed down the hall, he spotted Eddie walking into Room 11. He smirked as he looked down at his class schedule and noticed that he was in the same homeroom. When he walked in and Eddie saw him, they both cracked up laughing, trying not to be too loud, as the rest of the kids were totally petrified of the very idea of being in high school.

Frankie took a seat right behind Eddie and said, "The Freshman City Championship is a fuckin' lock." They both laughed hysterically.

"Where the hell were you man? I was lookin' for you," Eddie said.

"I was outside talking to a few broads, none were as hot as Colleen though," Frankie said coyly.

Eddie just laughed and blew it off with a friendly warning, "Easy Morelli."

Frankie was from the old school, probably because he was raised by such older people. He was forever grateful to Eddie for going to bat for him at camp. Having his back now was his top priority.

These guys spent the first few months of their freshman year doing everything together. They were helping every kid in the ninth grade get through Sequential Mathematics I. By the time the end of September rolled around, Eddie had his own table in the cafeteria set up as a makeshift tutoring station.

Eddie was everyone's pal, and helped anyone who asked. He helped two kids on the varsity football team pass math and chemistry so they could stay on the team. People were astounded at how smart Eddie was. One kid, Billy Bruin, was being tutored by a senior, and valedictorian candidate, Jimmy Ingoglia. He started going to Eddie instead, and was able to maintain a high enough average to stay on fall baseball. Eddie never asked anyone for a dime. Kids would try to pay him or buy him lunch, but he never accepted. Frankie knew better than anyone, the guy genuinely liked helping people.

The thing Frankie loved is that everyone knew he was Eddie's friend. He would actually offer Eddie's tutoring services in exchange for kids playing a few sheets.

Frankie and Eddie were inseparable. They took over a corner of the cafeteria. Eddie was the perfect cover for Frankie too. The teachers in the school were so thrilled that there was a kid who was doing the Christian thing, helping others with their work. Little did they know that more than half of the kids were fuckin' gambling as soon as they were done getting help from Eddie.

About a month before basketball tryouts, Frankie and Eddie joined a local gym. Eddie joined to make sure he was in the best shape possible for what looked to be a good season, based on the amount of talented freshmen at St. Elizabeth's that year. Frankie joined the gym to look for new clients and try to get a little tail. The guy never lifted a weight, but from all of the bullshittin' he did with different girls and all of the sheet action he was taking, he was sweatin' his ass off every time they left there. Frankie enjoyed playing hoops but never applied himself like Eddie had. It just came naturally to him. He would be lethal if he ever worked on his game. Tryouts were in two weeks and neither guy was all that nervous about making the team.

BASKETBALL TRYOUTS WERE FUCKIN' RIDICULOUS. The gym was absolutely mobbed with kids. There are three types of kids who show up at high school basketball tryouts. There are the kids who are so good that the coaches, who have been scouting camps all summer, unofficially of course, know exactly who they'll be guarding by the time they play in some non-league Christmas tournament. These kids are always easy to spot. They come dressed in Nike T-shirts and baggy shorts from various camps they had attended the past summer.

There are other kids who are so bad, that they either come to tryouts just to make a few friends, or their parents just need a few hours to themselves, letting these underpaid coaches function as fuckin' babysitters for a while. These kids come dressed in ridiculous outfits like full NBA uniforms: shirt, shorts, the works, and they usually cap it off with a white headband, thinking this will help their chances of making the team. It never does, and most times they are cut right away, as soon as the coach tells them to form two lay-up lines and they sprint towards the fuckin' baseline.

The third type of kid is the one who opens a few eyes, and shocks the hell out of the coaches. A kid, who after the tryouts end, the coaches talk about all through lunch, trying to figure out where the kid came from.

When Eddie and Frankie walked through the door together, everyone knew who Eddie was. He had been invited to a ton of camps since he was a little kid, his father had coached in the area, and he was about six feet tall by now. Frankie though, was just a tall mystery, having sprouted two more inches since the end of September.

There were about a hundred kids in the bleachers and three freshman coaches out on the gym floor. There was one head coach, one assistant, and one kid who recently graduated, just helping out. Eddie and Frankie were two of the taller kids so the coaches decided to let them play against each other. The coaches had about three or four scrimmages going on at once, trying to weed out the kids who weren't as skilled. Everyone was focused on these two kids, Mullaney and Morelli. The coaches couldn't believe that they hadn't seen this kid Morelli before. Frankie went to one camp. That was it. He really didn't play in any summer leagues, and he sprained his ankle halfway through his eighth grade CYO season. He had a pure left-handed jump shot and he was fundamentally sound.

Frankie and Eddie both wanted Michael Jordan's number when the freshman coach, Tommy Luigi, passed out the jerseys on the first official day of practice. Frankie felt that since Eddie was slightly better than he, and worked much harder on his game, that Eddie deserved to wear number twenty-three. Frankie took number forty-five, Jordan's baseball number.

Michael Jordan's father was murdered in July of 1993. Jordan left the game of hoops for the 1993-94 season to play baseball for the Birmingham Barons, a Chicago White Sox farm team. Frankie felt, although he knew he would never actually meet Jordan, that both he and Jordan had something in common the way they lost their fathers, and that forty-five belonged on his back.

The ongoing joke between Eddie and Frankie over that fuckin' jersey number was probably something that occurred in just about every high school throughout the country. Jordan quit baseball the following season to come back and play basketball with the Bulls. Frankie was breakin' Eddie's balls, because when Jordan returned to play basketball, the guy wore his baseball number, forty-five, just like Frankie. Eddie was fuckin' furious, and Frankie would wear his actual game jersey to practice just to really rub it in.

Eddie got the last laugh next season though. Both he and Frankie had jumped right to varsity, and after Jordan had a bad playoff game against Orlando, Michael Jordan went back to wearing twenty-three. Eddie was so happy, but Frankie really didn't care as much. Frankie was pissed off at Michael Jordan for other reasons. Frankie was all about business. Frankie felt bad for all of the people who owned sporting goods stores and got stuck with all of those forty-five Jordan jerseys that would never be sold, and for the parents of the little kids on his block, who could barely afford to buy a jersey for sixty or seventy bucks, but just did so to put a smile on their kids' faces. Most kids wanted to wear whatever Air Jordan wore, so there were many who got fucked by Jordan's "Superman move," switching back to the once retired twenty-three.

Frankie went out and bought himself a home and away Jordan jersey, with the forty-five on the back. He would tell the younger kids on the street that they could only play hoops with the older kids if they wore that same jersey that their parents got them, just to make the adults feel good. Frankie bought a dozen forty-five jerseys to hand out, just in case a few kids' parents couldn't afford one.

As the hoops season progressed, Frankie was making money. He had more than fifty guys who bet with him on a weekly basis through the sheets. He was very careful. He never gave a sheet to any basketball player, ever. He knew he had to keep business and basketball separate. He only distributed the parlay sheets in the cafeteria during the week, between 8:15 am and 8:30 am, and he never handed them out personally. He would keep them in a binder and place them on the table under a coat, someone else's coat. Money was passed once a week, on Mondays, using that same binder on the table.

Most of his teammates wanted to play the sheets, but Frankie would just tell them to go somewhere else. He knew that if one of these guys got caught, they'd choose ratting him out before getting kicked off basketball. The only kid who Frankie would let turn in a sheet would have been Eddie, but

Eddie had no interest. Frankie knew that running these sheets was good money, but this wasn't enough for him, and it was too easy. He wanted more.

One morning, about a month before the Super Bowl, Frankie approached a group of wanna-be-wise-guy tenth graders. There were about fifteen of them. They hung out at the same table every day, never leaving each other's side. They were a mixed group of Italian and Irish kids from various neighborhoods in Brooklyn and Queens. St. Elizabeth's attracted kids from everywhere, and these guys found each other right away. Out of the six daily classes on their schedule they had been in four of them, together, every single day. They drove some teachers to early retirement and they caused more shit in that cafeteria than any group of tough seniors in the school. One of the kids in this group, Niall Donovan, did a little investigative work during their freshman year. He was told that all they had to do was sign up for the sophomore male choir, and that would automatically place them in the same gym class as sophomores. These guys couldn't sing a fuckin' note. They just did it to be together.

Their gym class was given the name "The Goodfellas" by their Phys. Ed. teacher, Barry Raleigh. Raleigh was the new gym teacher and had been assigned to these guys for one reason and one reason only. Nobody else fuckin' wanted them. Raleigh thought that seeing this bunch together looked just like the table scene in the *Goodfellas'* movie, where Joe Pesci smashed a wine glass over the restaurant owner's head, and the rest of the crew just laughed. These kids were barely controllable. Thank God Raleigh was a bit of a lunatic himself. His hot temper was the only thing that kept these crazy bastards in line.

They were wild. They played sheets, took action among themselves, and bet every NBA game. They were the only sophomore gym class that would show up in a full gym uniform, with their beepers stuffed in one sock, and their cash rolled up with their football sheet in the other.

The Italian kids all looked the same. They had guido haircuts, earrings, and gym shirts with the sleeves cut off. The Irish guys all had red faces, long hair and bad cases of teenage acne. This group looked like a bunch of convicts in a prison yard when they were playing in gym class. They spent half of the forty-minute period cursing each other out. They took every game so seriously, probably because they had action on those games too. They spent the other half sitting on the side-line because Mr. Raleigh had to discipline them for their foul language over and over again. For some reason, he was the only guy who had any type of control over them, but not without it costing him a few bucks. Sometimes, if he ended up getting them on a Friday, he would have to buy them pizza and soda, just to keep them calm. The last day of the week was torture.

Most kids at that age would get their favorite teacher a card at the end of the year. Not these guys. They got Raleigh a brand new Knick sweatshirt, and a stack of five-dollar bills totaling $205, dumped a Gatorade cooler on him and told him to have a great summer.

Mr. Raleigh used to run a lacrosse tournament each year on the last day of school, called "The Raleigh Cup." He went out and bought a giant trophy, about three feet high, with the words "Raleigh Cup," written across the bottom. Below that was a blank plate, which would list the winner's names of the First Annual Raleigh Cup Championship. This event started off as a small game, but eventually evolved into one of the biggest events at St. Elizabeth's. The sophomore boys would show up in uniforms that they made, eye black under their eyes, with a pack of sophomore girls hanging out on the other side of the fence rooting them on. Sophomore year is one of the toughest on a kid to begin with. Losing the inaugural Raleigh Cup was something that the Goodfellas were not gonna let happen. They not only won the Cup that year, but three of them, Hayden Hennelly, Sal Modica, and Rob Cardi, were so fuckin' excited, that they offered Mr. Raleigh a hundred bucks each to bring the fuckin' Cup home for the summer. Raleigh turned them down, of course, but settled on letting the little maniacs drink from the Cup, using Pepsi instead of champagne.

The Goodfellas were getting bored with just trying to pick four for four on a weekly sheet. The bookie they all used to make their regular bets had them come to Staten Island on Thursday nights to settle up. Not having their driver's licenses yet made it a real hassle, so when Frankie made his pitch to them, they started betting with him.

Frankie capitalized. He got all of their action, and although they were very young, they paid up when they lost. They had a lot of respect for Frankie too. The very first week, this guy Eric Carillo hit Frankie for eight hundred, by betting a two-hundred-dollar reverse in the Duke-UNC basketball game. Frankie didn't flinch.

A reverse is 4-1 odds, and you have to hit both to win the full pot. Duke was laying 3 ½ and the over/under was 152. Duke won 78-76, not covering and taking the game over. Eric had bet UNC and the over. Frankie wanted to make a good impression on his new and active crew. He knew word would get around. Frankie showed up on Sunday morning at the bagel store where this kid Eric worked. He handed him eight hundred bucks in an envelope and said, "I always settle up right away if a guy wins that much." Frankie knew the school cafeteria was not the place to settle up with that kind of money.

FRANKIE'S BOOK KEPT GETTING BIGGER and bigger by the time he started his sophomore year. He had his pal Beckenburg working as a runner in Bensonhurst. Runners are the guys who meet people to either collect or pay out. They make their money when the gamblers lose on the bets that they placed with the bookie. The worse the gamblers do, the more the runners make. Period.

Frankie had a few kids running for him in school, and at the midway point of his second year of high school, he was the bookmaker for all the high schools within a ten-mile radius. He found runners in each school. He took action on just about any type of game. He was so busy, he would sometimes have Christina call his coach and tell him that he was too sick to make practice, just because he had collections to make, or payouts to attend to. He was only fifteen years old and was clearing about a grand a week, after paying his small staff. He loved the money he was making, but strived to do more.

Frankie never took too many chances. He had a great thing going and he didn't want to fuck it up. He began making friends with some of the older kids in the neighborhood who were taking their own bets as well. He didn't really give a shit about any of the games that his classmates and friends took so much of an interest in, he was more interested in the fuckin' money. He would always try to set his betting lines so that no matter what, he always made money. If kids ever started to load up on one team, Frankie would carefully try to move the lines accordingly, just so he could have half of his players betting one way, and the other half, the other way. If it got too out of hand on one side, he'd simply lay off his action to one of the older bookies. As long as he could make money on the vigs, he was happy.

For you Boy Scouts, a "vig" is a term that bookies use. It's like interest that a bookmaker charges a person who gambles. It's usually an extra ten percent tacked on to what the gambler loses.

Frankie had close to seventy-five kids betting with him now. Most of them were playing on a weekly basis, some of them would play three or four times a week. By the time his sophomore year ended, he had close to a hundred kids playing, and he was making more fuckin' cash than he knew what to do with.

FRANKIE WAS A HELL OF a ball player, but his right hand needed work. Eddie was constantly breaking Frankie's balls to take hoops more seriously, so he made Eddie a deal that he would walk home from school, everyday, dribbling a basketball with his right hand only, keeping his left behind his back. One day, Frankie was walking home from school on the jogging path by the Verrazano Bridge, dribbling a basketball, in the pouring rain, with his left hand swung awkwardly behind his back. Eddie wasn't there to supervise, but a deal was a deal when it came to those two. Rain or shine, Frankie made sure he kept his promise.

As the ball was bouncing into puddle after puddle, Frankie was concentrating on looking up while he was dribbling. He noticed a guy standing there, under a black umbrella, about fifty yards in front of him. At first he wasn't scared, but he did think it was strange that a person would be just hanging out by the water in that kind of weather.

Frankie put the ball under his arm when the guy stepped in front of him to block his path. The guy looked as if he was in his late fifties or early sixties. He was about five-seven, 180 pounds, with thick eye-brows, a wide nose, and a tan like he'd been at the fuckin' tanning salon and someone locked him in the tanning bed as a joke. He was wearing a copper bracelet and a pinkie ring. He wore a black overcoat, gray slacks, and a black pair of Reebok sneakers. He looked more like a fuckin' bus boy or a funeral director than a guy that Frankie would be scared of. "You Frankie Morelli?" asked the guy.

"Who wants to know?" asked Frankie. Frankie had his hair slicked back with a half a bottle of gel in it that day, and he wiped his eyes clear of the raindrops and wet gel that was running down, staring at this overcooked, little man, and laughing to himself.

"I hear you got some little empire goin' for yourself," said the guy, with a curious tone in his voice.

"I don't know what the fuck you're talkin' about." Frankie tried to pass the guy and continue dribbling, still having no idea who he was. He actually started to get a little nervous, and just wanted to get home. The guy let him get about ten feet and yelled out to Frankie.

"Your dad was a buddy of mine."

Frankie froze for a second before turning around. Now he was scared. He was young when his father died but he knew that most of his old man's associates were either loan sharks or fuckin' taxi drivers. He was never anyone's "buddy." Frankie was figuring the guy was coming to try to collect on one of his father's old debts.

The rain was coming down very heavily now and the two of them were standing there looking at each other. Frankie really had no idea what the hell the guy wanted.

"Relax, kid. I'm serious. He really was a friend of mine. My name is Nino Grilli."

Frankie tilted his head to the side, thinking he'd heard the name before, but not really too sure of who he was, or if in fact, the guy was telling the truth or not.

Frankie extended his sticky, soaking wet hand toward Grilli. "Well, nice meetin' you Nino, I gotta get home though."

"Wait a sec, kid. We gotta talk," said Nino.

"Listen, guy, if my father owed you fuckin' money or somethin', I can pay you. That's not a problem, but do me a favor, don't stand there in the fuckin' pourin' rain and act like you and my dad were fuckin' pals, alright? Now what the fuck do you want from me?"

Nino was cracking up laughing. "Well if that ain't a chip off the old fuckin' block. You got a hotter temper than your pop, kid. Truth is, he owed me a few grand when he was killed but I wasn't chasin' him down for it, nor am I askin' you for it now. I told him to pay me when he could. Wasn't the first time I let him slide either. Now, you gonna let me finish talkin' or you gonna keep cursin'?"

Frankie had a little smirk on his face. "Sorry, I have a dirty mouth sometimes. What do you want with me?"

"I'm here for two reasons," said Nino. "The first thing is that I just wanted to say how sorry I am about what happened to your father. I saw it on the news the day he was murdered and I felt awful, even a bit guilty. He may have been a bit of a fuck-up Frankie, but he really wasn't a bad guy. If it wasn't for him I probably wouldn't have any fuckin' teeth in my head. He

125

was always coming to my rescue when we were in high school and saving me from getting my fuckin' ass kicked."

Frankie's eyes were filling up but he didn't want to let on that they were. The falling rain was hiding his tears as Nino continued.

"Secondly," said Nino, "I'm here for business. You may not realize this, but you're becoming quite the fuckin' action taker, my friend. That's how it happens, man. You start out passin' out a few fuckin' parlay sheets, and before you know it, you're collectin' fuckin' thousands."

Frankie had an idea where he was going but he wasn't too interested. He liked running his own show. "Yeah, well, I can handle myself just fine," said Frankie. "Again, nice meetin' you. If you want the money back that my dad owed you, I can arrange that. How much did you say it was?"

Nino Grilli just kept talking. "I'm lookin' to move down to Florida soon, Frankie, and I could really use a bright young kid like yourself to come and work for me. If you're okay with just takin' bets from your fifty or so guys, well then that's fine, but…"

"A hundred or so," interrupted Frankie.

"Whatever," said Nino. "The point is that I'm not really askin'. After all, you're takin' action right in my backyard, and most guys would get their fuckin' ass kicked for that. I've been watchin' you for a while, though. You're intelligent and very organized, and frankly, I really have no choice but to lay low right now. I don't really want to get into it. You know Jack Sheridan and Luca Truglio right?"

"Yeah, I know em', why?" asked Frankie.

Jack and Luca, two local college sophomores, had been runnin' for Nino since they were Frankie's age. Frankie knew them

126

from playing pick-up ball at Dyker Beach Park from time to time in the summers. They were both students at Kingsborough Community College and they started to take notice of Frankie after they found themselves losing most of Nino's local high school action to Frankie. Luca was average height, with light brown hair, brown eyes, and a tattoo of the map of Sicily on the back of his left calf. Jack was shorter, about five-six, with dark hair, small dimples on each cheek, and a deep voice.

Nino's first reaction, when Jack and Luca made him aware of this fuckin' little prick stealing food from his kid's mouths, was to have someone either put a fuckin' bullet between his eyes or have a couple of guys from his crew scare Frankie into rethinking his newly found livelihood. It didn't take long for Nino to put two-and-two together and realize that Frankie was the son of the one-time clean-up hitter on his baseball team at P.S. 31. He decided to confront Frankie himself.

"Look, Frankie, you can still keep all of the guys that you deal with now. I'm not gonna bother you about them. In addition to them you can come in and work on a quarter sheet basis with me, just like I do with Jack and Luca."

"What the fuck's a quarter sheet?" asked Frankie.

"You get twenty-five percent of what the guys in my current book lose, that's all. Any new guys you bring in, we'll split them right down the middle. I really want you to think about it, Frankie. Listen, Jack and Luca are my youngest guys, but they're a lot fuckin' hungrier than any of the other guys I got workin' for me. I have a feeling that you are twice as hungry as they are. Shit, I heard you run that fuckin' deli like a prison. We take a lot bigger action than the shit you take. My guys are fuckin' *whales*, they bet thousands, kid."

"Whales" are guys who bet like fuckin' lunatics. Most of

Frankie's guys were just too young to bet really big. Frankie had so many of the small-time gamblers, that it was adding up and he was doing pretty well. A whale would be the type of guy that if he was down a grand or two, he'd fuckin' send it in for five G's without even blinking.

Frankie thanked Nino for the offer, but said that he preferred to do everything himself. He headed home that night, feeling certain that turning Nino down was the right decision, but unable to sleep, thinking about how much more fuckin' money he could make. Nino Grilli never used the words *watch your back,* when he parted company with Frankie that day, but he gave him a look that made him think, and he let Frankie walk away, unharmed, knowing that he had gotten his attention.

By THE TIME SOPHOMORE YEAR ended, Eddie stood six feet five inches tall and was a superior basketball player to Frankie, and just about everyone else. They already won consecutive city titles, but lost in the varsity state finals in their sophomore year. Eddie's sights were focused on three things: a state championship, college and girls. Frankie had been dating Colleen now for over a year, and they were crazy about each other. Frankie fell in love with Colleen the first time he laid eyes on her, and they started dating her first day as a freshman at St. Elizabeth's.

Eddie spent his whole summer looping and playing basketball. He played on just about every summer league team he could find, and he was getting better and better. He had already started putting aside some of his savings so he could buy a car, so that by the time the next summer came along, he'd be able to drive out to the golf course on his own. He was starting to enjoy caddying, and the constant weight of a golf bag on each shoulder was making him stronger.

Even though he wasn't old enough to drive, Frankie was able to get a car from one of his "clients," Johnny O'Connell, a college kid from Breezy Point, who was interning at a small investment-banking firm on Wall Street for the summer. Johnny took the subway to the city, and if you've ever been to Breezy Point you would know that having a car is not only unnecessary, it's actually a pain in the ass. Johnny owed Frankie seven hundred clams, and Frankie needing a car like he did, found a way for Johnny to pay him back. Eddie had a summer league game in Rockaway that night so he went down to Breezy with Frankie to grab Johnny's wheels.

Breezy Point is a town full of a labyrinth of sidewalks with three bars to choose from, and a keg on everyone's deck for passers-by to drink from as they walk home from the beach. It was heaven on earth, with some of the nicest people Frankie had ever met in his life, and he loved going there to grab the car.

Frankie was always intrigued how a community that small could set a record for Budweiser sales every summer. On an average Breezy Point morning, you're more likely to see the Budweiser delivery truck than the fuckin' mailman.

Johnny didn't have much of a choice but to surrender his car to Frankie after being on the losing end of Game 1 of the Knicks-Pacers Eastern Conference Semifinals. Reggie Miller dropped eight points in 16.4 fuckin' seconds, and the Pacers eventually went on to win the series. Frankie took the car as a payoff for that nightmarish gambling loss since he knew that Johnny didn't have any real money. You see, Breezy Point is "different." Down there, for high school graduations, parents give kids a case of Bud, cheese fries, and a foam beer coolie instead of cash, and the kids are fuckin' thrilled.

Frankie loved all of the action. It reminded him of his Uncle Fee's wedding. He loved watching guys yelling at televisions, fearing that if they lost a bet that they'd have him to answer to. Maybe it was that he loved the power, maybe it was just the money. Whatever it was, it was something that he craved.

Frankie watched Eddie's game and decided to make a quick stop over at Brennamendo's Pizza, in Howard Beach, right after the game. Brennamendo's Pizza was located on Cross Bay Blvd. This boulevard is one of the widest in Queens, with three lanes on each side and an island in the middle. The "Goodfellas" would go to Brennamendo's all the time, and they would never shut up about how great the pizza was at the fuckin' place, so Frankie and Eddie figured that they'd give it a try. There were a few Goodfellas and some kids from other schools who were late on their debts, so Frankie was going there anyway, hungry or not.

Frankie and Eddie pulled up across the street from the pizza place in Johnny O'Connell's blue 1992 Honda Civic, with their fuckin' knees pressed up against the dashboard. They weren't directly across the street, but back about a hundred feet or so, closer to the Belt Parkway. Eddie was just about to open the passenger side door when Frankie grabbed his arm to stop him.

"Wait, close the fuckin' door!" said Frankie.

"Why?" asked Eddie. "What's wrong?"

Frankie saw Nino's guys, Luca Truglio and Jack Sheridan walking out of Brennamendo's, each with a slice in one hand and a Snapple in the other. They were headed in their direction, but on the opposite side of the street. Frankie didn't want Nino to know he was anywhere near that place. Eddie had no fuckin' idea who anyone was but he just did as Frankie asked, without really asking too many questions.

"Let's just say that those two guys work for a competitor of mine," said Frankie.

Eddie just laughed. "You're like 'Sonny' from the fuckin' *Bronx Tale,* I swear to God man," said Eddie.

Frankie looked across the street and saw a hoodlum, wearing a backwards hat and more *bling* than fuckin' Puff Daddy, creeping up behind Nino's main guys with a fuckin' empty Colt 45 bottle in his hand, holding it by the bottleneck. Frankie was certain that the kid was gonna use that bottle as a weapon. "Holy shit!" yelled Frankie. "Stay in the car, Eddie."

As Frankie was half way across the street, Jack already had the bottle smashed across the back of his head. Luca had the cash they had just collected for Nino, close to twelve G's, stuffed in his dark blue Ralph Lauren shirt. Luca was just about to get the sharp end of the bottle when Frankie fuckin' nailed the punk in the side of the head, knocking his vintage 76er hat onto the sidewalk. Frankie had the kid on the ground, and he was beating the shit out of him, sending blows to his face, and filling up his knuckles with blood.

Luca pulled Frankie off of him, fearing he was gonna fuckin' kill him if he didn't. The kid just got up and took off after he realized that his only weapon was in a million pieces and he was completely outnumbered. Jack was lying there with a five-inch gash in the back of his head, and there was blood gushing down his neck and covering the Orlando Magic jersey he was wearing. Frankie, Eddie and Luca shoved Jack into the small car and drove him to Jamaica Hospital.

Luca was looking at Frankie and couldn't believe how he kept his fuckin' cool. Frankie was making sarcastic jokes as he was driving the car with one hand, and applying Eddie's T-shirt to Jack's head with the other. "You pricks owe me and my boy, Eddie here, a fuckin' slice and a Coke, mutha fucka!" said Frankie, jokingly. "Or at least an Italian ice, man."

Jack got twenty-seven stitches and was released around midnight. Frankie and Eddie waited in the emergency room to take them home.

Just as Frankie was dropping Eddie off in front of his house, he turned to Eddie and said "Yo, you look like shit bro, you're all fuckin' pale, we shoulda taken *you* to the fuckin' hospital. Get some sleep, Eddie boy, call me when you're done caddying tomorrow."

Eddie laughed, put out his fist for a quick pound, then gave Frankie the middle finger, in jest, and headed inside. "See ya tomorrow, Frankie, thanks for almost getting me killed tonight, bro, I enjoyed it."

MOST KIDS WHO WENT TO high school in the mid-90s got a taste of Yankee fever. New York schools were pretty much split down the middle, half of the kids were Yankee fans, and the other half rooted for the Mets. The Yankees' playoff run was pretty wild though, and with the Mets being out of it by then, the Yankees were the talk of the town.

The Yanks had waited a long time for a team like this. Derek Jeter just arrived on the scene and he was an outstanding young shortstop. A kid named Jeffrey Maier became famous in the fall of '96 when he helped turn Jeter's fly ball out into a home run against the Orioles. The kid reached over the right field wall and not only grabbed the ball right out of Tony Tarasco's glove, but pulled it over the wall for a Yankee home run. That umpire either grew up on the Grand Concourse, or just hated the Orioles because there was no fuckin' way that ball was a home run.

For the Yankees, and their fans, 1996 ended up being a very special season. Most people forget that during the opening day ceremonies for that season, the Yankee organization didn't announce the names of the players individually at the start of the game. Most fans assumed that it was because opening day was being played right through a snow-storm that year. There were rumors though, that the reason the players weren't announced was so Joe Torre and Tino Martinez wouldn't get booed out of the Bronx, having replaced two beloved pin-stripers, Don Mattingly and Buck Showalter. Although Tino had a rough start in the Bronx he came around, becoming one of the most well-liked and well-respected guys on the team. Joe Torre, despite the fact that when he arrived in the Bronx, the press greeted him with headlines that read "Clueless Joe," eventually went on to become a hero to just about every New York Yankee fan.

Eddie, like most Met fans, was rootin' his balls off for the Atlanta Braves in the 1996 World Series. He absolutely hated the Yankees with a passion, and would walk through the halls at school doing that fuckin' "Tomahawk Chop" every chance he got, just to piss off Frankie and the rest of his buddies that were Yankee fans.

On October 20, 1996, Andruw Jones, of the Braves, drilled not one, but two home runs off the Yanks in game one, becoming the youngest player to ever hit a World Series home run. Most Yankee fans that night were so pissed off, they were asking themselves, *"Who the fuck is Andruw Jones, and who the fuck taught him how to spell?"*

Eddie had been tutoring a kid named Keith Lorenz that year. Lorenz was a year older than Eddie and needed to pass math to stay on the football team. Football playoffs were coming up and Lorenz's father told him that if he didn't pass his mid-quarter exam, he was gonzo - off the team, no questions asked. Lorenz's father, Archie, a former Army boxing champ, All-American soccer goalie, and college professor, was a strict son-of-a-bitch. He was proud that his son was such a talented football player, but when he started slacking with his grades, Mr. Lorenz made sure he buckled down and got the number one tutor in the school. He was so excited when his kid passed his test, that he wanted to do something nice for Eddie. Mr. Lorenz still had some connections from his soccer days with a local ticket broker named Johnny McFogarty. Johnny hooked him up with two beautiful seats to Game 6.

Even though Eddie was the furthest thing from a Yankee fan, he was touched by Mr. Lorenz's gesture. He knew there was one guy who had to see that game.

FRANKIE WAS CLINGING TIGHTLY TO the silver pole in the center of the No. 4 subway train, as it pulled into the station at 161st Street in the Bronx. The train was packed with people chanting "Yan-kee Base-ball!" Frankie had forgotten how beautiful the stadium was. He and Eddie made their way down the L-train platform. There was a smell of *dirty water dogs* and shiskabob in the air, and a T-shirt vendor on every corner. They tried to sneak into Stan's bar for a few beers, but got fuckin' laughed at by the burly bouncer at the door. The game was in an hour, and Yankee fans mobbed the streets, chanting "Let's Go Yankees!" at the top of their lungs. There were about four hundred cops who lined the streets under the elevated subway as the fans got ready for the best night in the Bronx since 1978.

Frankie made Eddie take his picture as he headed through the Yankee Stadium gate, all decked out in Yankee gear, yelling, "Chop this, mutha fucka!" to the few Braves fans who they came across. Eddie got a great shot of Frankie getting his ticket ripped by the usher at the gate, as he winked at the camera.

Frankie wiped away a few tears that made their way down his face as he walked through the corridor by their first base line seats. He was thinking about his dad, and how much he would have loved this. He swore that he would never go to Yankee Stadium again, having only been there once before with his father holding his hand, switching seats every half inning to avoid the people who were chasing him. He was glad that his best friend forced him to change his mind.

Frankie and Eddie's seats were right on the first base side, in the main box section. They sat right next to Mike Francessa, the sports radio talk show host from WFAN, and were flattered when Francessa leaned over and asked them how the St. Elizabeth's team was looking for the 1996-97 season, telling them how he recognized them from the clips on Mike Quick's high school sports show, which aired weekly on the MSG channel. They felt like celebrities and couldn't believe that *he* knew who *they* were. Francessa was nice enough to sign their programs, and even took the time, during his next show, to mention them and wish them and the rest of their team good luck for the upcoming hoops season.

The Yankees emerged victorious, winning the World Series in six games. Yankee closer, John Wetteland, was swarmed by his teammates on the pitchers mound, as he cried tears of joy, and pointed his index finger straight in the air. Yankee third baseman Wade Boggs was riding on the back of a NYPD horse in center field. The horse part was the only thing about the win that Eddie liked, but he was glad to see his friend so happy.

Joe picked the boys up at the McDonald's down the block from Yankee Stadium.

"Eddie boy, I cannot thank you enough bro.   That was the best fuckin' night of my life," said Frankie, as he stuffed a hand full of French fries into his mouth. "Oops, excuse my language Mr. Mullaney." Frankie was bright red for a second, but he got over it.

Frankie was so glad that Eddie had thought of him when he was given the tickets. Frankie was happy he got to revisit Yankee Stadium. He understood why his dad loved the Yanks so much.

THIS YEAR WAS IT! THIS was the year St. Elizabeth's was taking the state championship. Their team was fully loaded and ready to play.

Eddie and Frankie had the best summer. They threw keg parties all summer and had a ball. The two of them were burning the candle at both ends. Two nights a week they would host huge bashes down at the beach where they had tons of friends. Frankie and Eddie would charge five bucks a person, all you could drink. This was chicken scratch to Frankie but he loved helpin' Eddie out. Frankie would almost always insist that Eddie keep his share. These guys would take the bus, train, or whatever car Frankie got his hands on from Brooklyn to Rockaway Beach every single night. Colleen and Christina would tag along. Colleen and Frankie were the main item at school. Frankie's sister, Christina, was about five-three, 110 pounds, with bright blue eyes, and a perpetual tan. Eddie was really digging her, but she really just liked him as a friend. The four of them were never apart.

Nino knew what Frankie had done for Luca and Jack. He made Frankie an offer that he couldn't refuse. He was grateful and to show Frankie his appreciation, he moved Luca and Jack to Staten Island, and kept Frankie in Brooklyn to handle all of his own guys, as well as over two hundred of Nino's. He saw in Frankie what most guys couldn't see, and he knew that this kid would be able to handle the pressure of keeping a book this big. He also figured that nobody would suspect a thing, and that Frankie would fly perfectly under the radar. Luca and Jack would have moved to fuckin' Buffalo if Nino told them to, but they were genuinely happy that Frankie was coming on board, and grateful that he saved their asses. They didn't care about crossing the Verrazano Bridge every day.

Nino Grilli spent most of his time on his horse farm in Florida, leaving everything in Frankie's hands. He would come back to New York two or three times a month, and meet with various members of his crew at a small Italian restaurant called Massimo's, near Prospect Park. Frankie would speak to Nino on a daily basis, using the disposable calling cards that Nino supplied all of his guys with. Frankie would always call him from a different payphone, and he would never use one that was close to the wire room.

Frankie walked into a great situation, keeping his own guys, and cashing in on twenty-five percent of what Nino's guys were losing. Nino's guys bet so much, that the quarter sheet deal that they agreed upon, was a sweet one. Any new guys that came in, they would just split their losses fifty-fifty. Nino trusted Frankie. He produced in a big way, and Nino made sure he was protected.

Nino's book was filled with guys who gambled huge amounts of money, and Frankie handled all of their action. There were some whales who bet five or six thousand a game. They had no idea they were placing their bets through a fuckin' kid. Frankie never thought that he would walk into something like this. There was one guy, a doctor, who bet twenty-five grand whenever there was a big boxing match. Frankie was taking bets from all kinds of people: union workers, cops, firemen, school teachers, and mailmen. His uncle's friends even started using him to place their bets. He also got calls from lawyers, doctors and a ton of Wall Street guys.

Frankie Morelli, the high school bookie, was fully in charge. He had the guys from the local Brooklyn bars, the bread-guy at the deli, about ten or twelve sanitation guys, and even his old Little League coaches. He even had the fuckin' Mr. Softee Ice Cream guy playin'. One summer, the guy couldn't pay after losing on the Phillies/Pirates game. Frankie made him give Christina, and every fuckin' kid on the block, a free double swirl cone with rainbow sprinkles right through Labor Day.

Frankie was making so much money. He had hiding spots everywhere. The deli, the apartment, various safe deposit boxes. He was fuckin' loaded, and very sharp. He always had the numbers in order, and he definitely needed to. He took some huge action. He made his money on the vigs, and always laid off the bets that he couldn't financially handle. He had been doing it that way for a long time, and nobody did it better.

Frankie always wore the same type of clothes as the other kids. He was never too flashy, except when it came to Colleen's gifts. He had Colleen's parents convinced that he was the highest paid deli clerk in America.

Eddie was doing pretty well for himself too. The members at the golf course where Eddie worked loved him. He used to run to the golf balls for them, with two heavy bags on his shoulders. He was a hustler, and all that looping kept him in incredible shape. Each day, riding the train back to Brooklyn, he would get down on the ground and do sit-ups and push-ups between stops. The people on the train were scared shit of this guy. He would go back and forth each day, except Mondays. Most private clubs are closed on Mondays. Those days he'd spend all day playing basketball or working out.

When school started these two guys were "the shit." They had about twenty or thirty keg parties throughout the summer. They kicked ass on their summer league teams. They were numbers one and two in the junior class academically, and with the state title being the goal, they couldn't wait for hoops to start.

Frankie was about six-three, 210 pounds, and Eddie made him look small. Eddie was about six-six, and about 215 pounds. They had an old-school coach name Tom Reardon who really knew his shit, better than any coach around. He was about six-two, with a full beard and shoulders as wide as a football field. He had a full head of brown hair turning gray, and a guttural voice that people feared. He had these guys ready.

Their team was comprised of the Morelli-Mullaney one-two punch, along with a little white sophomore point guard, named J.J. Freda, who played on the freshmen team and then jumped right to the varsity. Eddie and Frankie had done the same thing when they were freshmen, so they made sure that they took Freda under their wing. Plus they both wanted the fuckin' ball, so being this guy's friend was to their benefit. Their center was a kid from Bay Ridge named Mike Previti, a six-eight brick-shithouse of a catcher for the St. Elizabeth's baseball team who Coach Reardon had finally talked into playing hoops as a junior. Mike was born Michael Vincent Previti, and to his old man's delight, he just happened to have the initials MVP, and boy was he gonna have to fuckin' play like one for the next few weeks. There was no way Eddie and Frankie could do this by themselves. They needed Previti to be as tough on the court as he was when he was blockin' home plate on the baseball diamond. There was a tall black kid from Far Rockaway named Randy Samuels, who made up their starting five, and they had a sixth man named Mickey McManus who played on Eddie's AAU team. Mickey was the spark off the bench and always held the fort down when he entered a game. The team was solid, and if there was a year for them to win the state title, this was it.

They breezed through the regular season that year, capturing their usual Brooklyn-Queens championship. They were ranked number one in the Brooklyn Diocese and the city championship was a joke. In the championship game they handily crushed St. Raphael's 75-51. They were on their way to the "Big Dance" as many of them called it. The game was in a week and they had some tough practices ahead of them.

WHEN THE TEAM GOT OFF the bus up at the Pepsi Arena in Albany, they looked just like the kids in the *Hoosiers* movie. Scared shit. They knew they were good, but the team that they were about to face hadn't lost a game in two seasons. Frankie played the two-guard position and Eddie played small forward. Everyone was hoping they would be on, just like Hickory's Jimmy Chitwood.

They all read *Street and Smith's* magazine regularly and watched films for a week before the game. They knew what they were up against. The team they were playing, St. Patrick's from upstate New York, was the number one team in the country. They started four huge black guys, three of whom came from the same area growing up. They had been playing together since they were four years old. They also started a six-three white kid from upstate. This mutha fucka could jump out of the gym. Frankie was going to have to guard this kid who had the court sense of a John Stockton, and went after the ball like Charles Oakley. He was mean, tough, and very sound. Frankie pretended, as he always did, not to be afraid.

When they walked into the gym on game night, they had pits in the bottom of their stomachs. Their opponents looked much more confident. St. Patrick's was located in Glens Falls, New York, and was twice the size of St. Elizabeth's, so they had more kids to choose from. The refs hadn't entered the gym yet, so the players from St. Patrick's were putting on a dunk fest, throwing down reverse slams, and tossing fuckin' ally-oops to each other like they were playing a game of "Horse" in the schoolyard. It looked like a fuckin' NBA dunk contest. That feeling of being the underdog was starting to show among the St. Elizabeth's team.

Well-known rap artist, Notorious B.I.G., a.k.a., "Biggie Smalls," had just been killed two weeks prior to the championship game. He was always popular, but it seemed that his music took on even more popularity after his death. Even adults knew his rap songs. "Hypnotize," was the hot "Biggie" song at the time and that song was crankin' throughout the arena, while the St. Patrick's guys were throwing down one dunk after the other, chest-bumping each other, and even chest-bumping some of their fans who were seated in the lower rows. The St. Patrick's fans were singing the words to the song in unison. The St. Elizabeth's players just walked along the baseline, single file, with their mouths wide open, looking as if they had seen a ghost.

Frankie was trying his best just to calm these fuckin' guys down. Eddie just kept looking up at the huge scoreboard. Last year's state final was held at Fordham University, in the Bronx.

It was just like going to a regular game. This was different. This was like playing in a pro game, and the team they were playing looked like the Chicago Bulls.

Frankie grabbed his teammates and huddled them up. "Yo, we're better than these douche bags, you hear me?" asked Frankie, waiting for agreement in the eyes of his teammates, but not getting it. "We can beat these mutha fuckas. Now come on!" The guys were starting to respond. They all yelled, "DEFENSE!" as they broke apart and headed for the lay-up lines. They were nervous, but starting to get pumped.

St. Elizabeth's sent fourteen fan buses packed with students and faculty. The school band was compiled of a hundred kids, and every single one of them was there. The Mullaney's had driven up with Colleen and Christina and they were all decked out in St. Elizabeth's gear. The cheerleaders and step squads were going back and forth at each other with different cheers. Every one of those crazy Goodfellas was there, taking action on the game, most likely. The kids on the team didn't care if they were doing that or not, they were just impressed that they all made the trip. They were too cool for the fan bus thing, so they got their own bus. They even hired fuckin' DJ Blinky Jamin, an up and coming white rapper from Beach Channel High School, to play the tunes for the ride. All of them had their matching green and white T-shirts off like the Duke fans at Cameron Indoor before the tip-off. They each had at least a dozen beers in them, and they had the St. Elizabeth's side of the arena fuckin' rockin'.

The Albany police were scattered in two's around the court, after the riot that occurred eight years ago between two state rivals. Albany cops always made this night part of their detail. This was about as rowdy as the place could get without the police calming things down. The room was at a fever pitch.

Frankie and Eddie were the team captains. They made their way out to center court to shake hands with the other team's captains and meet the referees while Coach Reardon was prepping the rest of the team in the huddle. Frankie and Eddie were not even looking at the three referees. Their eyes were glued on two of the opponent's captains who they were about to battle. Both guys were black. One guy was a senior on his way to North Carolina. He was about six-ten, 230 pounds. The other guy wasn't as bulky, but stood about six-nine, with hands the size of a fuckin' first baseman's glove. He was also a senior, and he was attending Florida State the following year for both basketball and football.

St. Patrick's had one other captain who had been off to the side and appeared to be getting a few last second words of encouragement, but not from his coach. It looked as if he was talking to his father in the stands. The refs motioned for the kid to get out on the court and he started to make his way toward them.

Eddie had his eyes glued on this particular player. He had watched film on this guy and he told Frankie exactly how to guard him. He even forced Frankie to watch a little film too, feeling Frankie had a great chance against the kid, due to their similar styles. Eddie was looking at this kid, but Frankie wasn't. Frankie was staring in the face of the man who the kid had just finished talking to. Frankie knew he had seen him somewhere before. He walked away from the huddle of refs and players and started to walk toward the stands. Frankie got a bit closer, and his heart sank. Fuzzy McGlynn was sitting in the stands.

Frankie couldn't believe it. He had to make sure that it was him. His hair-style looked different, and he no longer had the beard, but Frankie swore it was him. When he got close enough to see that shamrock tattoo on his neck, he knew it was Fuzzy. Killing people was what Fuzzy did, and he was so blasé about it, he had no idea why the hell this kid was so focused on him. That day he shot Frankie's dad was just part of his daily work, as far as he was concerned. He didn't even know Vinny Morelli had a son.

Frankie watched all of that film on this kid in preparation for the game. All he knew was that he was going to be guarding a kid named Gooch Duffy. Fuzzy McGlynn never married, and Gooch used his mother's name. After Gooch's mother had passed away, Fuzzy made his way north to Glens Falls to try to blend in with a regular society and hide out from all of the crime that he had built his life around. He was trying to creep his way back into his son's life by acting like a real dad sitting in the stands. Gooch Duffy had already received letters from almost three dozen Division I schools so McGlynn took an extra interest in his newly found fatherhood career, hoping that one day he'd be able to profit from his kid's talent. He arrived at the Pepsi Arena very early to watch warm-ups and made sure that he stayed on the St. Patrick's side. He knew his kid was playing against a Brooklyn school, but felt it would be highly unlikely that any of these hard-working, tuition-paying parents would recognize a guy like him. Never did he think a fuckin' kid would make him.

Frankie's grandfather had saved all of the newspaper articles written about his son's murder. Frankie stored them in his shoebox and read them every year on the anniversary of his dad's death. McGlynn was never arrested for killing his father, but his face was all over those articles as the lead suspect.

McGlynn's face was burned in Frankie's mind. Frankie had no doubt that this was his dad's killer, sitting fifteen feet away.

The crowd was going nuts as the captains started to walk back to their benches. Frankie was in a cloud. Suddenly he didn't give a shit about the game anymore. He was enraged, and shaking like a leaf. He had to guard the kid who just got a last second tip from his father before the biggest game of his life. Frankie's father had never even seen him take a lay-up.

Coach Reardon was screaming, "Hey Morelli, get the hell over here!" Frankie looked as if someone just ripped the life out of him. He could see Reardon yelling but everything was in slow motion. He had no idea what to do.

Eddie ran out and grabbed Frankie by the arm, "What are you doin' bro? What the fuck is wrong with you?"

Frankie put his hand on Eddie's shoulder. "Eddie boy, I'm gonna fuckin' lose it, kid!"

Frankie was scared. He looked up at Colleen and Christina. They both looked so cute in their dark green sweatshirts that read, "LET'S GO LIZZIES." The arena was so fuckin' loud and the game hadn't even started. Frankie looked dazed, seeing all of these people who traveled so far to watch his team play: all of his friends, the Mullaney's, the school band, and all of his teachers. The players made their way out of the huddle and everyone walked towards the guy who they were going to be guarding in the game so they could exchange a quick fist pound or a handshake. Previti took his spot for the jump ball, giving a half- hearted good luck handshake to the St. Patrick's center.

The referee never even got a chance to throw the ball up. McGlynn's kid extended his hand toward Frankie. Frankie looked at his hand, and then sent one of his classic head butts right into his fuckin' face.

Frankie didn't just break the kid's nose. He managed to fracture his cheek-bones on both sides and damage his right eye socket. Frankie finished him off, with a quick kick in the mouth, as the kid was lying on the floor. There was blood spattered on the faces of the few kids who were lined up close to Fuzzy's kid, and the black and white shirts that the refs were wearing were sprayed with spots and lines of red.

St. Patrick's fans ran out onto the court before security could do anything to stop them. They were followed by the St. Elizabeth's fans. Fuzzy McGlynn came running to the aid of his son. Eddie and Previti tried to grab Frankie and get him out of there, but the cops got him first. They handcuffed Frankie before he could even move away from the Pepsi logo at center court. Joe Mullaney told Kathy to stay back with the girls and then limped his way out onto the floor. The Cheerleaders from both teams were hysterically crying, and parents were holding their kids close.

As the cops were dragging Frankie out the door, he was screaming and crying at the same time in McGlynn's direction as he was lying on the floor with his kid, "You mutha fucka, that's what you get you son-of-a-bitch!"

The scene on the court was out of control. The game was cancelled immediately.

The handcuffs were so tight on Frankie. The cops were fuckin' pissed. They would probably have been more sympathetic if they knew the reason behind Frankie's rage. Nevertheless, they were tough on him.

The fans were confused and peppering each other with questions about what exactly happened. The cops escorted Frankie out of the gym and placed him under arrest. Joe Mullaney could not figure out what just made Frankie snap. Joe told Eddie, the team, and Coach Reardon, that he would find out where they were taking Frankie and go there.

The game was postponed until the next morning. No fans permitted.

S̲ᴛ. Pᴀᴛʀɪᴄᴋ's ᴘᴜᴛ ᴀ ʙᴇᴀᴛɪɴ' on St. Elizabeth's the very next day. They were just tough and angry enough to pull out the win, despite the fact that their star point guard was laid up at Albany Medical Center with multiple fractures. St. Elizabeth's was undermanned, but believed they lost because they didn't have Frankie on the floor. The guys on the team were really pissed off at Frankie. He had averaged 22.7 points and nine assists per game that season. Frankie would have made a huge difference and his temper cost them the game. Frankie knew it too, and he felt awful.

Eddie had heard every story over the years about the death of Frankie's dad. Eddie saw how it killed Frankie when Eddie's perfect family would show up at all of their games. He knew that's what Frankie wanted in his life, too. That was part of the reason why the Mullaney's loved Frankie so much. He really appreciated the time he got to spend with them. They were like a family to him.

Eddie really wanted the state championship title, but he couldn't hold that against Frankie. He would have probably done the same thing if he had been in Frankie's shoes.

Frankie spent the night in Albany in a small, dark holding cell. He was allowed one phone call, and instead of calling his grandparents or his uncles, he called Richie Beckenburg and told him to cover the office until he got out. Sundays were busy in March with all of the college basketball games going on. He thought about calling Nino, but knew that he would probably be fuckin' pissed off, so he decided to wait until he got back home.

Kathy and the girls went back to Brooklyn on one of the fan buses. Joe went to the police station in the morning and bailed Frankie out. They drove back together in total silence until they reached the Tappan Zee Bridge. As they were driving over the bridge, Frankie's tough guy image was starting to break down. He looked over at Joe and started to cry. Joe just leaned over and rubbed his head, "It's not the end of the world Frankie, you'll be fine."

"I'll probably get expelled, right?" asked Frankie.

"Who knows? I'll talk to Brother Stanley and explain everything, maybe he'll understand," said Joe.

"Ha!" cried Frankie. "You don't know that guy too well, do you? They're gonna toss me."

Joe figured Frankie was right, but he was humoring him by being optimistic, telling Frankie he'd give it a shot. Frankie's eyes were watering a bit, as they crossed the bridge from the Rockland to the Westchester County side, and he looked towards Joe.

"Mr. Mullaney, do you know how I met your son?"

"Sure, at basketball camp, of course I remember. I had to drive about ten miles out of my way that day for you," said Joe, with a smile on his face.

"Did you know that I showed up at camp, thinking that I was hot shit, excuse my language, and he stopped two guys from kickin' my ass?"

"Come on, my Eddie?"

"Oh yeah, you're little Eddie beat the shit out of these kids, and they were his friends too. He didn't even know me yet."

"No Frankie, I didn't know that," Joe said solemnly.

"Mr. Mullaney, I'm really not what you think I am. I really don't think I have been the best influence on your kids. Your son is my only real friend in the world, and I love your daughter with all my heart."

"Frankie, you have been dating Colleen now for about two years, and both of my kids spend every single minute of their lives with you. I let them do that because I trust you. Spare the confessions, kid. You think I'm a fucking dope?"

Frankie was surprised to hear an F-bomb exit the mouth of "Mr. Do-no-wrong."

"I know deli clerks don't buy diamond bracelets," said Joe.

Frankie felt his blood turn to ice. He was stunned.

Joe continued. "I tried to tell Eddie to bring you down to the caddy yard to start looping. I told him to tell you how much cash he was making, how it would keep you in shape, and how much you would love it. He said that you made a lot more money than he did. Hope you don't mind kid, but my kids spend their entire lives with you. I had you checked out a bit, and I know about the bookmaking. I also knew your father."

Frankie spit out his orange Gatorade all over the dashboard

of the Mullaney's car. He was shocked at what Joe said. At first he just assumed that since he was an ex-cop, he must have met his dad in some prison somewhere. As Frankie was using his sleeve to wipe off the dashboard, he started to laugh a little.

"Well how about that. You lock one Morelli up and then bail the other one out, crazy huh?" Frankie snickered.

Joe looked at him and smiled. "Frankie, on the day that Eddie was born, I had just gotten started at my new job in Manhattan, after having worked in the Bronx for five years. They gave me some piece of shit car that broke down on the side of the West Side Highway with a flat tire. It was a cold December day and I was stuck there with no gloves or anything. I was freezing to death. I was nervous. I was a kid, with a new job, in a brand new area, and the guy with me was even younger. I didn't even have a warm coat or a freakin' tire iron in the car. I flagged the first car I could find. I saw a cab coming and started waving desperately."

Frankie was turned completely around in the passenger seat, staring straight at Joe the second he started speaking about a cab.

Joe continued with his story. "Your dad got out, tire iron and jack in hand, and he ordered us to wait in his cab while he fixed the car. He knew how cold we were and he pulled over right away. I tried to help but he took care of it, and he also handed me the cup of coffee that he had just bought himself."

Tears were rolling down Frankie's "tough-kid" cheeks. He was still somewhat confused, and part of him thought it was some bullshit story that Joe created just to cheer him up a bit, but he didn't really care if it was or not. This had been the first time that he had heard a nice story about his dad, and he was enjoying it.

"Your dad got the flat fixed in a matter of seconds. My partner took the car back so I could head home to take Mrs. Mullaney to the hospital. Your father gave me a lift to Penn Station and we spent the whole trip talking about the births of our kids. Both of our wives were due any minute. We were just two guys excited about being fathers for the first time. Just shootin' the shit, having a few laughs, and talking about what we were gonna name our kids. It's funny, you weren't even born yet, but he was hoping for a boy so bad, he was already calling you 'Little Frankie.' I saw him again on the news a year later when he was killed. He had a face that was unforgettable."

Frankie snickered.

Joe continued. "I always wondered what happened to that kid of his, remembering how excited the both of us were that day. I finally put it together the Christmas before last. Colleen asked me to take her to the mall to buy you both a Christmas and birthday gift, commenting that you had the same birthday as Eddie."

Frankie spoke very slowly, with tears still on his face. "Well, I'll be a son-of-a….."

Joe interrupted. "Let me tell you something, Frankie, that cabbie's kid turned out okay. You're a great friend to my son, and you treat my daughter like an angel. I'd prefer that you didn't do what you did, but that's up to you my man."

Frankie was speechless, still choked up a bit, completely floored by what he had just heard, but happy to hear such a nice story about this confused and misguided father of his. He looked Joe right in the eye, with a puzzled look on his face, "When did you know…."

Joe cut him off. "I had a feeling you were involved in betting when you and Christina were at the house last year for Thanksgiving. I asked you if you liked cranberry sauce and I was holding the dish up in your direction. You know what your answer to that was?"

Frankie was smirking, "No, what?"

"You took the plate from my hands as you were staring into the living room, not paying a bit of attention to me, and you said 'Detroit's givin' two and a half.'"

Frankie was doubled over laughing. Joe was actually laughing too.

"Is that when you ran a check on me?" asked Frankie.

"No," said Joe. "That's when I got suspicious. Constance Hall is when I knew for sure."

Frankie looked confused. "Huh? What do you mean Constance Hall?" asked Frankie, still smirking.

Joe was smiling too, knowing that Frankie knew exactly what he was talking about. "Colleen had signed up with St. Elizabeth's to go to the Constance Hall Nursing Home during the holidays to volunteer. Mrs. Mullaney or I would drive her there. She would go with a few of her friends and they would feed the elderly people, read to them, that kind of stuff. One day after I dropped her off, I was pulling out of the lot."

Frankie was laughing, knowing what he was getting at already.

Joe continued. "I looked up and I have to say, I was stunned to see you there on Easter Sunday morning at 8:00 am, heading into the nursing home. I was so curious, that I parked the car and followed you inside. I stayed back so you wouldn't see me. After you went into the elevator, I walked over to the woman that you had just signed in with. She was an elderly Spanish woman…."

Frankie cut Joe off. "Hmmm yeah, that's Miss Rochelle, she was a doll."

Joe was chuckling, dying to go on. He continued. "I asked the woman. You see that kid in the Knick jacket who just walked through the elevator?"

"The woman said, 'Of course, that's little Frankie. He takes the bus here every Sunday. The old folks love him. He's been coming here since he was in grammar school. Take a ride up with me, you gotta see this kid with these old men.' "

Frankie was proud of himself and somewhat embarrassed that he got caught doing his weekly good deed. Frankie spent two years going to that nursing home, and always waited across the street for Colleen and her friends to go in first. He would go in right after them, and stay there for hours. He never even told Colleen what he was doing. He had no idea that anyone knew about it until now.

Joe told Frankie how he took a ride up on the elevator to the 6th floor. This was the floor where the majority of male residents lived. Many of them had no families.

Frankie laughed as Joe continued. "I got off the elevator and I could not believe what I was looking at. I saw about twenty-five elderly men, most of them in wheelchairs sitting in the hall, wearing Knick flannel pants, real Knick jerseys, and some of the guys were wearing Jordans. Miss Rochelle told me that you wanted your floor to look like the real team, and you bought all of that shit with your own money. You were sitting there with your back to the door. The McDonald's High School All American Game was on TV and I overheard you taking action on the Met game at the same time. That's when I knew what you were up to, and I wasn't all that happy about what you were doing, but it's also when I realized that my daughter had met someone very kind."

Frankie thanked Joe for bailing him out, for making him feel great about his dad, and for making him feel great about himself.

"Mr. Mullaney, I promise you that I will try to cut down. I can't promise that I'm gonna stop takin' action all together, but I will cut it down. There's no freakin' way I'm goin' loopin' every summer morning like your crazy son, but I will tone the bookmaking down. I just hope that I can stay at St. Elizabeth's for senior year. Mr. Mullaney, seriously, thank you."

Joe smiled and dropped Frankie off at home. Frankie just smiled and walked into the apartment.

JOE MULLANEY DID EVERYTHING THAT he could to try to prevent Frankie's expulsion, but he was unable to convince the principal to let him stay. Frankie was expelled immediately and was forced to finish out the rest of his junior year at the local public school in Brooklyn. It was nearly impossible to tone down the bookmaking now, even if he wanted to. He was already the most reliable, organized, and popular bookie in all of Brooklyn and Queens, with almost four hundred regular clients, between his guys and Nino's. He had completely gotten out of the football sheet scene by now, having passed it down to the younger brother of one of the Goodfellas. He figured that was a smart move, and that the new generation of Goodfellas would be fuckin' delighted. He was making Nino twice as fuckin' rich as he already was, and Nino wanted him to continue to stay focused.

It was March of 1997, beepers were going out and cell phones were coming in. Frankie purchased a cell for Eddie, one for Colleen, and another one for Christina. They never lost touch. They went to different schools, but nothing changed, and they all still hung out every weekend. Colleen and Frankie were still dating. The beach parties were the best now since most of the seniors were old enough to pick up the kegs in their own cars. They upped the party fee to ten bucks per head.

One night, Eddie brought a few of his caddy pals from Long Island to Rockaway Beach. They called themselves "The Brewski Crewskis'." They all loved Frankie. They thought he was the funniest mutha fucka in the world. They couldn't get over his generosity. He used to stand over by the kegs and yell out, "Yo, these guys here are Eddie's loopin' buddies, whatever the fuck that means, and they are our guests. Plus, I would never let a FLID pay for beer at one of our keg parties."

The Brewskis' all raised their glasses to Frankie to thank him. Little did they know that FLID stood for, "Fuckin' Long Island Dick." Frankie was breakin' their balls, and they knew it, but they didn't care. They drank all of the beer on the beach and none of them minded getting called a "FLID." The Brewskis' were a great bunch of guys and still hang out together all of the time. Brian O' Dwyer, leader of the Brewskis', rents a bungalow in Rockaway every summer. He competes in the bagpipe contest every August at the Irish Festival. Every Brewski member is there each year to root him on. They were always glad that Eddie introduced them to the area. Rockaway is their favorite vacation spot in the world.

Frankie's new high school, Andrew Jackson, made business a lot easier. Frankie could have set up a desk in the hallway with a sign that read, "Bookie Here." The school had metal detectors at every door, graffiti on every locker, and chains on the gym doors. The school security guards had too much shit on their plates to be worried about a little white guy takin' a few bets. Most of them would bet with Frankie anyway, vig free too. Frankie was no dummy. He once had this big security guard, Lester, crying his eyes out because he lost eighty bucks on the Stanley Cup Finals. When Frankie got to school that day, he said, "Hey Lester, you know nothin' about fuckin' hockey, bro, stick with bettin' hoops. I'll tell you what, I'll let the eighty slide if you just keep watching my back."

Lester was relieved that he was off the hook on the eighty dollars and he never bet hockey again. He also made certain that Frankie conducted his business without ever getting hassled.

On Frankie's first day at his new school, he saw kids telling teachers to fuck-off. There were fights in the hallway. Teachers would actually avoid walking near certain punks. There were kids screwing in the bathrooms. Frankie was in shock, but tried to act like a bad ass. He knew a lot of kids in the school, and the ones that he didn't know, knew who he was. He was a two-time city champion at St. Elizabeth's, and he felt that all he had to do was act like it and he'd be fine.

The fuckin' kids at this school bet on anything. One kid lost fifty bucks on a boxing match and couldn't pay. Frankie made him come to the deli and work a full day folding the Sunday papers.

Frankie's office accepted any bet. When you called in, you had to give an account number and a password. If you didn't owe any money and you were under your limit, you could play horses, boxing matches, baseball, basketball, hockey, anything. Anything you wanted to bet, you could bet with Frankie.

Every Sunday night he would tally up the work for the week, bring the tape recordings to a separate safe in the deli basement, and shred all of the paperwork. Colleen never really got involved, but she really enjoyed the perks. After Frankie's little conversation with Joe, Frankie always made sure Colleen was never anywhere near him when he was working. He had so many guys working for him at this point, it really didn't matter. He could oversee his business with a cell phone and lounge on the beach all day. Actually, sometimes he did just that.

THE "BELMONT STAKES" IS JUST about as sacred a horse race to a Long Islander as "The Kentucky Derby" is to the people in the Bluegrass State. The race takes place in June, at Belmont Park, and the people who show up there are more interested in drinking beer, than watching the fuckin' horses race. Anyone who lives within ten miles of the racetrack has "The Stakes" circled on their calendar likes it's fuckin' Christmas. There's always a story every year about a husband and wife who spend the whole week prior to the Stakes arguing because they have to miss the event. It's usually when an out-of-town family member throws a graduation party or a wedding that day, and the cocktail hour starts right about the time they open the starting gate. The fight usually ends after the Stakes is over. Unless of course that horse, who the husband was definitely gonna bet, wins the race and his wife never let him stop at OTB to place his bet. Shit, June is the most popular month for divorce filing anywhere east of the Cross Island Parkway.

People start lining up outside Belmont on Stakes day at about 6:00 am looking to capture a picnic bench or a grassy area to set up shop for the day. There's always the standard six-foot hero, full kegs of beer and the occasional TV. Most of the attendees are dressed in clothes that they already know they will never wear again, anticipating a day of cheering, pounding beers and capping the night off with a keg-stand if they should happen to win the big race.

There's a crew of about thirty people from Floral Park, New York, a small, incorporated village that borders the racetrack. This group shows up each year dressed in matching T-shirts, with a funny catch phrase on the back. Two Stakes' regulars Matt Connolly and Diane Mannle work on the shirt phrases for weeks, trying to find the most fitting one. This particular year the phrase was an easy one. "Silver Charm" was look- ing to capture the first Triple Crown since "Affirmed" in 1978. Connolly and Mannle had their group ready, all decked out in shirts that read "Three Times a Silver Charm." There were over seventy thousand people at the park waiting to witness history, hoping for the Triple Crown. Bruce Beck, from "Sportstalk," would always drop by each year to get footage of the group in their funny shirts. Some years he'd even wear one and inter- view the rowdy bunch before the big race.

The T-shirt group always sets up next to one of the biggest parties in the picnic area. This Belmont party is an infamous one, and is hosted every year by none other than Uncle Fee and Uncle Louie.

Frankie gave Eddie strict orders to make sure that he lied to his parents about looping that day so he could catch the Stakes.

Frankie's uncles had over two hundred people at their party. They had about thirty cases of Bud, five kegs of Coors Light, a Sabrett hot dog umbrella, a face painter for the kids, a magician, a clown, and each kid got a giant horse balloon. There was a DJ crankin' the *Let It Ride* theme song right before each race.

Frankie was actually taking live action from Fee's friends late in the day. The lines at the betting windows were long. Plus, a lot of the guys were just too drunk to stand in line anyway.

Fee and Louie had two friends who would always be the first guys at the track on Stakes day. One guy "Nicky Eyeballs" would spend the entire day with his large eyeballs glued to the *Daily Racing Form*. Nicky was the fuckin' best handicapper in Floral Park and loved giving a horse or two to the drunks who were just there for the kegs. The other guy, "Tommy Lips," would call every single race with his binoculars in hand, flapping his lips better than the announcer, Tom Durkin.

Eddie had the best day of his life. With his height, he got a chance to see every race clearly, and he even got a chance to visit the barn. Nino Grilli owned a few horses that he kept at the stables at Belmont. One of Nino's exercise riders, Cliff Capelli, bet through Frankie from time to time and Frankie let him slide on the $350 he owed him, as long as Cliff would give Eddie a guided tour of the stables.

Silver Charm lost that day, and another Triple Crown had slipped away. Eddie didn't care though. He set a record for fuckin' keg-stands, doing six of them, shot-gunned ten beers, and even hit the exacta that day. It was Eddie's first Belmont Stakes, and he was already planning his lie to his parents for next year as he and Frankie stumbled home on the train. Eddie vomited several times on his way home. His face looked as yellow as the beer he had been drinking all day. He still managed to get up the next morning. He somehow found enough energy to make two loops that day to make up for the one he missed the day before.

ASIDE FROM THE TALL BLONDE who walked around screwing one guy after another, the 1980 movie *Caddyshack* was pretty damn close to the real thing. Down at Eddie's yard, there were great loops, shit loops, heavy bags, nice light bags, great straps, straps that were like fuckin' fishing string, hard-workin' likable kids, scumbags who stole loops by kissin' ass, drug-free kids, kids that smoked at least two doobies per loop, young caddies, old caddies, rich ones, poor ones, tall loopers who picked up the bags with ease, little guys who would drag the bags on the fairway as they walked on it, smart guys, and guys as dumb as Carl, the Bill Murray character. There were also some members who were as sincere as Chevy Chase and knew a smart kid when they saw one.

Eddie was very well liked. This was his fourth summer there and he loved it. He had just purchased a 1966 Mustang convertible with the caddy money he saved. The car was red with a black interior, bucket seats, and had a 289 V-8 under the hood. The grill on the front had a beautiful horse on it. This was probably ninety percent of the reason why Eddie loved this type of car. He started working two summer jobs that year. He would get up each day at 4:30 am, head down to Aqueduct Racetrack to walk the horses for an hour, and then shoot out to the caddy yard. People were always amazed at how much energy the guy had. The guys at the barn loved him. He used to bring donuts every Friday for all the other hot-walkers. He loved working with the horses, but realistally he could only work there a few hours a week because he was making great money looping.

Eddie became interested in Wall Street after talking to some of the older caddies everyday about the market. He would devour the *Wall Street Journal* while waiting for a loop. Soon Eddie caddied for guys and gave them stock advice. Some of the members thought he was talkin' shit but many times he'd use his mathematical prowess to predict great performance in an unknown small cap stock.

One day, he was lucky enough to caddy for a young member named Brian Quinn. Brian was a sharp-lookin' guy, about six-one, 190 pounds, with black hair and an off-the-boat, Irish looking face. This guy was the best loop in the club. Every caddy would "hang the rail" when this guy showed up. He wasn't the best golfer in the club. He was just above average playing to about a fourteen handicap, but he was a good guy who called the caddies by their name and always, unless a kid totally fucked the loop up, tipped like a maniac. This guy was throwin' kids fifty bucks for his bag, when other guys were tossin' twenty-five or thirty. It wasn't because he was showing off or trying to make the other guys in the club look bad. It was because he was an ex-caddy, who had made it in life. That's what the kids looked up to, and Brian was the type of guy who they wanted to loop for.

That morning, Eddie and Brian were walking down the fairway, just bullshittin'. Eddie had caddied for Brian before and always tried to dazzle him, like Charlie Sheen did when he bought Michael Douglas those birthday cigars in the *Wall Street* flick. He loved trying to blend in with the rest of Brian's foursome when they were discussing business. Brian would frequently play with a big redhead, named Dennis Kavanaugh, and he and Brian would laugh to themselves about how hard this kid was trying to rush his life away, trying to be like them.

Brian would usually pretend to blow Eddie off when he started throwing stock talk around, but he was casually paying very close attention. He was actually somewhat impressed that the kid was reading the "Journal," of all papers. Brian was also a basketball coach in his town on Long Island and he followed the high school basketball circuit pretty closely, so he and Eddie had a lot in common.

Eddie and Brian were on a first name basis. Brian was a father of four and he admired Eddie, even though he thought the kid was starting to fuck around a bit too much lately. As they walked towards Brian's tee shot on the third hole, talking about a bunch of things: hoops, the competitive Rockaway summer leagues, the run up at Rucker Park in Harlem, the upcoming season, that type of shit, Brian looked at Eddie and said, "You like looping, Ed?"

Eddie replied. "Well...yeah I love it, especially now that I have a car and stuff. It keeps me in shape and I am actually really starting to like golf."

Brian had a smile on his face but he had just enough seriousness in his tone to make Eddie listen closely. He looked at Eddie and said, "Don't fuckin' jerk my chain, Mullaney, and fuck golf, I fuckin' hate golf, I'm just playing because the golf course is a great place to do business. Now stop telling me what you think I want to hear."

Eddie put the bags down, shocked by Brian's tone. "I'm really not too sure where you're going with this Brian, I mean...."

Brian cut him off. "Eddie, you're a good kid, I like you, and I think you're a great ball player with a ton of potential. You'll probably do awesome in a low to mid-level Division I school, maybe even a top D-I program if you have a decent year this year."

Eddie was glued to Brian's face. "Okay, but?"

Brian continued, "You're gonna have to do something for me, Eddie. My nephew, Ray, goes to St. Elizabeth's. He told me that you have been number one in your class for the past three years. He also told me that you and your fuckin' wannabe gangster friend run the best Rockaway keg parties every weekend. You're pounding beers every weekend night, I can smell the booze when I see you here in the mornings, and I know that you're driving drunk all the time. I guess what I'm saying is that, eventually, everything catches up with everyone, and you need to start thinking about the future. I was born in Brooklyn too, and I did the same shit, Eddie."

"Remind me to have a little talk with your nephew," said Eddie, sarcastically.

Brian continued. "From now on, if you have the car with you, no more drinking and driving. You took trains and buses your whole life, leave the car where it is if you're too fucked up."

"Brian, I promise, I will ……..."

"Shut up, I'm not finished," snapped Brian.

Eddie tucked his chin into his chest and whispered his apology under his breathe, "I'm sorry."

"Eddie, I will talk about the stock market with you anytime you want, but it's not going to be here, it will be from across a desk. Next summer, I want you to come to work for me at the hedge fund that I run downtown. I have already figured that you probably make anywhere between five and six grand working here for the summer, is that about right?" asked Brian.

"Yeah, it's pretty close to that," said Eddie.

"Well I'll pay you seven thousand dollars next summer to work as an intern for me before you go to college. It's a foot in the door, and there's nothing but ex-basketball players workin' in my office anyway, so your fuckin' stooge ass should fit right in. Oh, and I will also pay for your lunch each day too, on top of the seven grand. You better make sure you keep in shape though, because Wall Street guys eat like wild animals. This kid, Timmy, who works with us, he's like fuckin' seven feet tall, makes you look like a shrimp, and he has filet mignon every fuckin' day. As far as the boozin' while you're driving shit goes, well I have a question for you."

"Okay?" asked Eddie.

"What did you get on your SATs, about fifteen hundred or something?" asked Brian.

Eddie smiled, so proud of himself. "Fifteen-forty, sir," said Eddie.

"Oh yeah? Well congrats. You're the perfect fuckin' Channel Four news story when you drive your convertible off the

Marine Park Bridge one night because you've had too much to drink. If you don't cut the shit, you can bet that's what will happen. These news crews love a great lead story about a smart kid who 'could have made it' if he wasn't so careless."

Eddie had his head down as he was walking up the fairway. He was embarrassed, but he thought it was cool that this guy not only wanted to give him a shot, but he took the time to care. He could handle being yelled at. He had played for Coach Reardon long enough to know that the yelling has its purpose.

Eddie smiled and looked up at Brian, "I gotcha Brian, and thank you for the opportunity. I would love to intern there. I saw how well Sully has done working for you. He was kind of a fuck-up too. What's the deal, you got a soft spot for fuck-ups?" Eddie laughed at his own comments.

Brian looked at Eddie and smiled, and said, "No problem, just make sure you don't fuck it up. Oh and by the way, you didn't get this loop today because you're a great caddy. I called Freddie and told him to assign this loop to you because I wanted to speak to you. So don't start thinking you're hot shit." Brian laughed at himself, and walked down the fairway.

Eddie was flattered. His dad was right. The caddy yard is a place where connections are made. He couldn't wait to get home and tell his father the great news. He actually even stopped at Blockbuster and rented *Wall Street* on the way back to Brooklyn.

FRANKIE ADAPTED TO HIS NEW school very well. It was actually a much better set-up for business. Since he was no longer a student at St. Elizabeth's, he had handed off most of the St. Elizabeth's work to a junior there named Mark, from nearby Howard Beach. Mark had some racket. This guy was the most generous kid at St. Elizabeth's. He'd buy lunch for everyone in the cafeteria, treat everyone to cheeseburger deluxes with cheese fries at the diner after a drunken night of city clubbing, and cart kids around in his Benz. Nobody could figure out why. At first, everyone thought the kid was a drug dealer. It turns out, that this guy had been collecting a check for a grand a week from a winning "Win For Life" ticket. The kid hit the scratch-off game as a freshman, and he was too young to claim it. He had his older sister go to the Lotto office and say she won and he paid her two hundred clams a week to keep her fuckin' mouth shut. He kept the rest. Frankie figured that because everyone knew about the "Win For Life" story, the teachers would least suspect Mark, so Frankie had him running that end of the business.

Frankie's local business was booming. He took over Nino's office completely. The office was located about three blocks from his grandfather's deli. Frankie set up a part of the office for his grandfather, so he could meet with his accountant once a month. That part of the office was just a front. It was set up to look like a storage room for the deli, and he kept it in the front end of the building. It was dark, with deli aprons, lockers, and old broken-down slicing machines that he purchased at a restaurant auction. It was so convincing his grandfather's accountant never suspected a thing.

Behind that office was a state-of-the-art wire room for bets to be taken. The place looked like Vegas. Frankie had a ten thousand dollar soundproof wall unit installed. There were about twelve guys working there during the busy hours. Frankie had done it right: a paper shredder at every work station and three phones on each desk. Flat screen TVs were just becoming popular and he had one of those mounted in each corner of the room. If anyone were to see this, it would be very hard to believe that a teenager could be in charge of something like this. There was a door leading from the front room, through a small hallway, right into a room where the bets were taken. He had Nino's guys working the weekends, and he brought his own guys in during the week.

The guys he had working for him were fuckin' grown men for Christ's sake. Some were recently retired, looking to make a few dollars. Others were working guys, picking up a few bucks on their days off. There were a few school security guards from

Frankie's high school who would even fill in from time to time. This guy had everybody working.

Frankie was the smartest kid in his school by far. He was in all advanced classes. He had accumulated enough college credits, which enabled him to have a light schedule. Most days he'd be done around 11:00 am. He would always use this as office time, to check in on the work coming in and head back for practice around 2:30 pm. His basketball team was decent, but nothing like St. Elizabeth's. He was the only white guy on the team, and he just didn't give a shit about hoops anymore. He never quit though, he always wanted to keep up his average high school kid appearance.

He had just gotten back from the mall, and after stopping by the deli to say hello to his grandfather, he headed over to the office to hide Colleen's Christmas gifts. He had gotten her a ton of shit: jewelry, a television, a pair of roller blades. He was sitting at the desk in the front office and got beeped by one of his phone guys next door. He walked in and was happy to see it was a busy day.

It was a Friday afternoon and most of the clients were just calling to check the early lines for the upcoming NFL playoff games. Some guys were betting the ponies from various race-tracks. The phones were ringing and Frankie was excited. He loved being in charge, especially at his age. When he started to walk around the room, guys would sit up straight, empty their ashtrays, dump their coffee cups out, making sure that their desks were neat. Frankie liked that they were scared of him. Frankie took good care of all the guys, and they were all happy to be working for him despite the age difference.

Early Friday afternoon is generally a slow time of the day for a bookmaker, so there were only about four guys there.

Two of the guys were in their mid-50s, each with a lit cigarette in their mouths.

One guy, Cal, was a friend of Frankie's grandfather. He used to work full-time at the deli. He loved answering the phones, but mostly he loved all the action. He was an average-size guy, with a ton of curly white hair, and a thick pair of Coke- bottle glasses. Cal's son, "Cotton Top," sat next to him, and he was the spitting image of his old man. The guy next to them, "Pinkie," was an out-of-work roofer, with a full head of jet-black hair, five-inch side burns, and a pink face. This guy looked just like a burnt Elvis. The last guy was Richie Beckenburg. He was now about six foot eleven. He could barely squeeze into the desk. He was the one who had called Frankie into the room where all four TVs had the same news channel on. Richie had a very concerned look on his face.

"What the fuck is wrong?" asked Frankie.

"They just arrested Fuzzy McGlynn," said Richie.

"Get the fuck outta here! Where?"

Fuzzy was now a suspect in four unsolved murders. When he killed Frankie's dad, there had been a bus driver who identified him through a photo. Frankie knew that the night he put Fuzzy's kid in the hospital was the cops chance to get this fuckin' guy, but he figured it was just too late. Fuzzy brought his kid outside the arena and threw him in the school principal's car telling them he'd meet them at the hospital, but he never showed up. Fuzzy knew, with all of Frankie's yelling and screaming, that he'd get caught.

"Beck, where the fuck did they get him?" begged Frankie.

Richie Beck responded. "They found him shackin' up with some broad in Jersey."

Frankie was in disbelief. "I cannot believe this shit."

Richie went on. "They mentioned your father and the murder of a guy Abruzzi or Abruzzo."

Frankie started to fill up a bit. He felt like he did it, like he was responsible for catching Fuzzy. For the last year, he had regretted crushing that poor kid's face. He always felt that it wasn't the kid's fault, but it was the best he could do at the moment. He also felt badly that he had let his team down. Today was the day that he stopped feeling that way. He was glad that he did what he did. "Did they say anything about…."

Richie cut him off. "Oh, one more thing. They also said that he was last seen at a basketball game in Albany. They said he had been there to watch his son play in a game, and had escaped before anyone could get to him. Sorry, Frankie, I tried to remember as many of the details as I could for you man, I even jotted a few things down here," said Richie as he looked down at his pad.

"No Beck, don't be crazy bro, you remembered everything man, thanks a lot," said Frankie.

The other guys were all just silent. They didn't know what to say. Congrats? Good Job? Frankie had been waiting a long time for this day, and they were just happy for him.

Christina was still a student at St. Elizabeth's, but she had been home sick that day. When Frankie called the house to tell her the news, she had already watched the whole thing. She was crying tears of joy when the phone rang. She knew it was Frankie who was calling.

Frankie went into the bathroom to throw some water on his face. He had to get himself ready to tell his grandfather. As he was coming out of the bathroom, there was a knock at the back door. He didn't even get his hand on the door handle.

Boom! The door was knocked in, tossing Frankie to the ground like a rag doll. There were FBI agents everywhere. There was a sea of dark blue jackets, glass shields, and guys with their guns drawn. They yelled, "Freeze, FBI, mutha fucka, stay the fuck down on the floor!"

Frankie had already been knocked to the ground. He was lying there, face down, with all of his phone guys lying right next to him. They tried to reach for the paper shredders, and shuffle shit under the desks. It was too late though, these guys had the place fully surrounded.

The office had about ten FBI guys surrounding it, but it seemed to Frankie like ten thousand. There was a guy stepping on the back of his neck, forcing his face into the carpet. The guy had the handcuffs on faster than fuckin' Houdini.

The head FBI guy entered the room a second later and started to read Frankie his rights as the other guy kept stepping on his neck harder and harder.

"Francis Morelli, you're under arrest, you have the right to remain silent."

The agent in charge continued as Frankie was lying there in a cloud. "Anything you say may be used against you in a court of law. You have the right to an attorney..."

As soon as the agent got right about to that point, Frankie was able to free up his neck and spin it around so he could look up. He was shocked at who he saw.

Joe Mullaney was standing over him with the Miranda Rights card in his right hand, holding it in front of him as he continued to read. He was wearing a dark blue FBI jacket, long dark pants, and a pair of sunglasses. Frankie was speechless at first, until they started dragging him out the door, when he began yelling in Joe's direction.

"You mutha fucka! You're a fuckin' Fed?" He was going fuckin' crazy. "How could you be a fuckin' Fed?" Frankie was kicking his legs as the agents were trying to cuff him. He continued to scream in Joe's direction. "You mutha fuckin' scumbag, cocksucker, mutha fuckin' lyin' prick!" He was crying and screaming at the same time. "I fuckin' hate you, Mr. Mullaney, you were like my father, you mutha fucka, I fuckin' hate you! How the fuck could you do this to me?"

As Frankie was being walked down the steps, Joe stayed behind to oversee the other agents, and the NYPD, as they were tearing the office upside down. The look of guilt on Joe's face was very apparent. He and the agents seized close to $300,000 in cash, and over $75,000 worth of paper action for the upcoming weekend. Frankie was headed downtown in the FBI van, still screaming and cursing at the agents driving the car.

The Feds had been watching Nino Grilli for a while. They knew he was involved in racketeering, and a ton of other shit that Frankie was probably not even aware of, but their case had dried up completely when Nino split town. They knew their best shot to find him was to try to break Frankie Morelli. They didn't know how much Frankie knew, or if he even knew where Nino was, but they were determined to find out.

Eddie leaned over the toilet at the St. Elizabeth's gym after taking a shot to his mid-section during practice. He was spitting up blood and his face looked as if he'd held his piss in for a month. He was completely yellow and his eyes were as white as a hard-boiled egg. Halfway through practice, Coach Reardon told him to pack up and head home after the kids started calling him piss-face. They were just breakin' his balls a bit, but Reardon knew that the kid was really hurtin'.

When he walked in the house and Kathy got a look at his yellow face and obvious jaundice signs, she took him right to the family doctor, Dr. Michael Lally. Eddie told her that he had taken a whack to the chest in practice, but she knew right away this was something more serious. Kathy was twirling her hair in the car all the way to Dr. Lally's office. She had started to notice the yellowish color in Eddie's face the past few weeks, but just thought it was because he was involved in so many activities, and that maybe he was just a bit run down. His coloring on this particular day was different.

Dr. Lally had been the Mullaney's physician for fifteen years. He was always supportive of Joe with his leg injury, and had taken very good care of Eddie and Colleen over the years. Kathy stood behind Dr. Lally as he was examining Eddie. She was twirling her hair quickly and biting her nails at the same time.

After the check-up, they sat with Dr. Lally in his office. "It could be a number of things, Kathy," said the doctor. "There is something called Gilbert Syndrome that can cause this yellow look. I'm not saying that this is what it is, but I have seen cases of it before, and these are usually the signs."

Just hearing the word "syndrome" made Kathy sit up straight in her seat and pull it closer to the doctor's desk. She started to jot down everything that he was saying on a pad that she was holding as the doctor continued. She asked Eddie to step outside while she began to ask Dr. Lally a few questions.

"This Gilbert Syndrome, what causes it? And how are we going to treat it?"

"Relax, Kathy," said the doctor. "Gilbert Syndrome is not life-threatening. It is a common, yet harmless condition where a liver enzyme is a bit abnormal. We need to check him for a few things. Jaundice can occur when a person is experiencing liver or gallbladder disease as well."

The word "disease" brought Kathy closer to the front of Dr. Lally's desk with tears streaming down her face as she leaned on his desk on her elbows, and continued writing down everything he said. He gave her the names of four or five liver and gallbladder specialists as they exited the office, telling her that everything was going to be okay.

"Hang in there," said Dr. Lally. "We'll see Eddie tomorrow for some blood tests and we'll take it one step at a time."

Dr. Lally hugged Kathy and they walked outside to see Eddie. The doctor reached up to Eddie and rubbed him on the head. He winked at Eddie, and said, "You'll be okay, kid."

Frankie and his attorney sat in a room at the far end of the FBI building in lower Manhattan. The office was set up as the main headquarters for all of the surveillance cases throughout the Bronx, Brooklyn, Queens, and Manhattan.

Joe Mullaney was a cop for five years in the Bronx, hoping desperately that he would get the FBI call. He started in the FBI office in lower Manhattan on the day his son was born. He was an FBI agent with his two good legs for all of eight hours before his accident, and he fought like hell through the courts, in June of 1981, to keep a desk job with the FBI when he was finished with physical therapy. Joe was the first person to win such a lawsuit prior to the *Americans With Disabilities Act Of 1990,* and spent the next sixteen years working undercover for the Feds.

Being an FBI agent had been his dream since he was young, but he never imagined that he'd be in the middle of something this awkward. Whether Frankie was like a second son to Joe or not, he still needed to do his job.

Frankie's grandparents, with the help of Fee and Louie, got Frankie a great defense attorney from Midtown named Tommy Culhane, a Bronx-born Irish lawyer with a blue collar background and a near perfect track record in these situations. Culhane had defended Mafia types and career criminals for over four decades and was certain he could knock these charges down to nothing. Frankie was still nervous, since he was on probation from his assault charge, but he was confident that he had the best attorney around. Culhane was about fifty years old, with brown hair and brown eyes. He wore a dark blue Armani suit with white pin-stripes and a sky blue and white checkered tie. He was sitting to Frankie's right with his briefcase in front of him, giving Frankie a pat of confidence on his back to try and put him at ease. He was the right guy.

Agent Mullaney walked into the room and sat down. He nodded his head at Culhane and looked in the direction of Frankie. Frankie was staring straight ahead, not even acknowledging his presence. Joe addressed Frankie's lawyer. "Mr. Culhane, can I have a few minutes alone with Mr. Morelli, please?"

Frankie interjected, "Fuck you, Mr. Mullaney! If that's your name, or maybe I should call you fuckin' Donnie Brasco, you lyin' prick!"

"Not another word, Frankie!" said Culhane.

Frankie ignored his lawyer and started to get more sarcastic with Joe. "Tell me, 'Big Joe the Cop,' are you gonna tell me now that my whole high school life has been a fuckin' farce and that my best friend and my girlfriend are fuckin' agents too? Go ahead I can take it, come on."

"Relax, Frankie, of course not." Joe was starting to get slightly teary-eyed. He felt awful about everything, and now he had to deal with his son's illness. Joe, on some level, realized that Frankie was the best thing that ever happened to his kids. This whole thing was absolutely killing him.

Ordinarily, a savvy attorney like Culhane wouldn't let his client speak to the arresting agents for fear that he would incriminate himself, but in this case, it appeared that Frankie was actually unnerving Mullaney, and Culhane liked where this was going.

"So how long?" asked Frankie.

Joe had his head down as he answered. "The Bureau has had you under investigation for about a year."

"The Bureau, what fuckin' Bureau? You mean you! You've had me under investigation. You phony bastard!"

"Frankie, you have to relax," said Culhane.

"No Frankie," exclaimed Joe, trying to get his word in. "It wasn't like that, let me explain."

"Oh, fuck you and fuck your explanations. I trusted you and thought of you like a father figure. You're a fuckin' scumbag!"

Joe had to tell Frankie the whole story and he needed him to listen. Culhane reached over and whispered in Frankie's ear, trying to get him to calm down.

"Frankie, will you listen to me now, please?" asked Joe.

"Call me Francis, my friends call me Frankie."

Joe started to raise his tone slightly and began to tell his side of the story.

"Nino Grilli had been under surveillance for years before I got here. He had been involved in everything: guns, drugs, organized crime, I mean everything. What they were watching in '86 was a huge drug ring that Nino was running during Met games. We worked together with the D.E.A and the N.Y.P.D and discovered that Nino had been strong-arming a *Harry M. Stevens* beer vendor into moving cocaine through empty beer cups for him during night games, so Shea Stadium was my assignment. At first, the Bureau wasn't going to let me stay on, but I fought like hell for desk duty. After that, they set me up at Shea, knowing that Nino's guy at the beer stand would never suspect a one-legged usher of staking him out. I am as undercover as they come, Frankie. My kids don't even know I'm an agent."

Frankie shifted in his seat.

Joe was getting worked up since this was a tough situation. He loved Frankie, he was like a son to him, but he had to do his job, even though he had way too much on his mind right now for any of this. Eddie had been diagnosed with *Autoimmune Hepatitis*, a progressive inflammation of the liver, causing acute liver failure. All Joe wanted was for Frankie to be scared enough to give them what they wanted so Frankie could maybe get out of this mess, but Frankie wouldn't flinch. He just sat there with a frown on his face, still in total disbelief that this man did this to him.

Joe continued, "Nino's drug ring dried up, and the beer vendor mysteriously disappeared about a month or two after the World Series. Nino Grilli was nowhere to be found for a long time, until about three years ago. We were never able to get him on anything. Then, eleven months ago, we found out that he was involved with you, of all people, and now we want to know where the fuck he is!"

Frankie was acting like he wasn't even listening. "I'm sorry, what did you say that guy's name was?"

"Look, Frankie, I'm not crazy about any of this shit, I was just doing my job. I mean, do you know what it's like to have everyone that I work with knowing every fuckin' detail about you and my son getting bombed four nights a week at the beach? Or how about the fact that every guy in here knows all of the details about you having sex with my daughter! This hasn't been easy for me either you know."

Frankie was beet red, but so pissed off, he didn't care how embarrassed Joe was.

"Fuck you!" screamed Frankie. Frankie was trying to keep his calm and cool demeanor as best he could by just tapping his fingers on the table and staring up at the ceiling, pretending to whistle right through what Joe was saying. As far as Frankie was concerned, he was just taking advantage of a great business opportunity working for Nino, and he didn't really care what kind of gangster shit Nino was involved in. Frankie was making more money than most of the grown-ups on his street. He thought Nino was the greatest.

Joe continued. "Look, Frankie, they have been tailing all sorts of people. Your pals Luca and Jack are downstairs right now."

Frankie shifted in his seat again. He remained pokerfaced, with a deadpan look about him. He was still staring straight ahead.

Joe just kept talking. "Frankie, when I saw your name come across the desk, I was surprised. If I could have jumped out a window to get away from all of this shit, believe me I would have. I mean, I knew you took a few bets from the kids at school, but Jesus, Frankie, you have no idea what kind of guy Nino Grilli is and you need to tell us where he is."

"Fuck you," said Frankie again. "I ain't tellin' you shit. I cannot believe you did this to me."

"That's enough," said Culhane.

Frankie whispered into Culhane's ear seeking permission to address Joe one last time. Culhane knew that he had already let Frankie talk way too much but he could see how he was getting to Joe. Culhane nodded his head at Frankie, granting him his wish.

"Mr. Mullaney," said Frankie. "I think you're an asshole, and I will never be able to respect you, ever again. That being said, I think your kids are the best. I love Colleen, and Eddie is my best friend. I don't know what the policies are here, but I need to see Eddie. I've been talking to him on the phone all week, and I have been avoiding going over there because of you. Well fuck that! I'm gonna go see him whether you want me in the fuckin' house or not. You don't have to worry, I'll put on a great show, they won't know how you stabbed me in the fuckin' back. I just want you to know that I'm not going away, not a chance."

Joe's eyes were filling up a bit. He was trying to be tough but he couldn't. "You can go and see Eddie. You're the only one that he's wanted to see anyway."

Frankie left and headed for the Mullaney's as soon as Fee and Louie posted bail for him. He and Christina spent the whole night with Eddie and Colleen. Colleen and Christina spent most of the night crying, and looking through pictures of the four of them at the beach the summer before, and some action shots they had taken of Frankie and Eddie during their basketball games throughout high school. Frankie spent the whole night telling Eddie that things were going to be okay.

Eddie's disease blindsided the family. The stress of just sitting and waiting to see if a liver transplant was going to be his only option was taking its toll on everyone. Donor livers are matched to recipients according to a number of different criteria. In some cases, family members can donate a portion of their own liver to a loved one, provided the person receiving the liver was of average height. This organ can regenerate and adapt to the body of the recipient. This was not going to be an option for Eddie, and he knew it. He read up on his disease, and he knew that if he was going to need a transplant, that he would be in real fuckin' trouble.

Frankie was in deep shit with the Law, but he didn't care about that. He was looking at this poor kid, sitting in bed, crying, and saying things that Frankie couldn't believe he was hearing. Eddie was talking about how bad he wanted to play college ball. St. John's was less than twenty miles from the house. Eddie loved watching clips of Chris Mullin playing for the Redmen in the '80s. The guy was his idol. Mullin was from Brooklyn, and had four wonderful years at St. John's, graduating to the NBA after that. The kid just wanted to have a shot at playing there too.

Eddie had been recruited by a few schools, but between his looping job, his friends and family, and the St. John's stipend check, he felt staying home was okay for him. He could save some money, caddy in the off-season, and still play at a good Division I school. His dream was to play at Madison Square Garden. He and Frankie had actually been chased out of the Garden when they were sophomores. They got so drunk that they ran across the court during a St. John's game against Connecticut and escaped before anyone could get them. Eddie had Frankie cracking up laughing as he was recalling that night when they were cheered by more than 19,000 people for being fuckin' drunk and stupid. Eddie was holding back tears and hoping that their childhood prank wasn't going to be his only time on that court.

Frankie tried as best he could to hold the tears back but he had a tough time. Eddie was very ill, and Frankie had a difficult time seeing him that way.

Frankie slept on the floor of Eddie's room that night. Early the next morning, he woke Eddie up and took him for a ride to Belmont Racetrack. It was about five o'clock in the morning when they left Brooklyn. Eddie had no idea where they were going. Frankie already had the whole thing set up for Eddie.

Frankie helped Eddie out of the car and had him wrapped up in a blanket. As they approached the practice track, Eddie's eyes lit up like a little kid on Christmas morning. He had walked hundreds of thoroughbreds before, but he never actually sat on one. People always told him he was too big. He took a short ride on a beautiful horse named *Ellie's Game Seven*, a name that Frankie knew Eddie would love. *Ellie's Game Seven* was an eight-year-old gelding that was retired about a year. Kenny, one of Frankie's clients, and the horse's trainer and owner, kept the horse around for good luck. Kenny was a degenerate gambler who was too superstitious to ever sell a horse with that name, fearing that he would lose all of his Game 7 bets for the rest of his life.

"This is fuckin' awesome, Frankie!" yelled Eddie. The horse was moving like a snail, at about two miles per hour, with Eddie aboard. Eddie's feet were practically touching the track, but he was having the day of his life. He was bent down, like a jockey, screaming like Tom Durkin, "And down the stretch they come!"

When they drove back to the Mullaneys' house, Eddie and Frankie spent the whole ride crackin' up laughing. "Now that was the scariest lookin' jockey I have ever seen," said Frankie.

Frankie had put aside his situation with Joe because he was so upset by how sick Eddie was getting. Eddie laughed for the first time in a week, and for just a little while, forgot all about his liver.

IT WAS SATURDAY NIGHT AND St. Elizabeth's gym was packed. It was the biggest gymnasium in the area and they needed as much space as they could find. Eddie had been on the donor list for a few weeks now, but the Mullaney's were just running out of time. If Eddie did not get a new liver in the next few weeks, he would worsen. The Mullaney's felt helpless.

Although the FBI had very good medical coverage which would pick up all of the transplant costs if a donor should arise, the people of St. Francis Parish and St. Elizabeth's High School still wanted to do something to ease this family's pain. Joe had already borrowed money against his house just so he could be liquid. He thought that maybe there was someone he could pay to move Eddie up on the donor list. He would do anything at this point. He was so fuckin' desperate, he cried day and night.

The whole neighborhood pulled together and organized a fundraiser at the school. Everyone who knew Eddie was there. Kids from school, all of the loopers who he worked with at the golf course, his basketball coaches, and his teammates. Brian Quinn and Sully showed up too, with a check for twenty thousand dollars from their entire office. This really boosted everyone's spirits. Frankie and Christina came with friends from Bensonhurst and Bay Ridge. There must have been close to six hundred people there. There was a silent auction, a 50-50 raffle, dunk tanks where teachers and coaches took turns getting dunked, a DJ, a band, and a buffet table forty feet long.

Eddie was not able to attend, his condition having taken a turn for the worse. He was at New York-Presbyterian Hospital, hoping and praying for a donor.

IT WAS ABOUT 7:30 SUNDAY morning. Colleen kissed her mom on the cheek and woke her up. She had dozed off in a chair in Eddie's hospital room. Colleen was telling her mom about how much money they raised the night before, and how many great stories that she heard about her brother. The fundraiser was a huge success.

After Eddie's freshman year in high school, he would spend every day of the week helping his friend Lew Bruns at his tutoring clinic. The clinic was set up to help the neighborhood kids in the eighth grade prepare for their high school entrance exams. Lew was a local cop and a math wiz. He was about seven years older than Eddie and had been his mentor for years. He helped Eddie prepare for his math bees. He brought Eddie on board because he just got too busy between his hours at the precinct and all of the kids he was tutoring. Together, the two of them helped over three hundred kids get into their high schools of choice. Eddie always got home later than all of the other kids from basketball practice. Nobody ever realized that the reason he was late every night was because he was tutoring. Just about every kid who Eddie and Lew helped over the years showed up at that benefit.

Joe was getting ready to head to the hospital before 8:00am as he did each day now. He heard a knock at the door and was surprised when he opened it.

"Mr. Mullaney, I wanna cut a deal," said Frankie.

"Where's your lawyer?"

"Fuck the lawyer," said Frankie. "This is between me and you, and I think there is a way we can save Eddie, too."

Joe looked completely puzzled, yet very interested at the same time.

"Come on in," said Joe. "Have a seat, Frankie. Thanks for everything you did for us last night. The benefit was a huge success, in large part, because of you. You brought so many people, and getting a hold of Mr. Quinn, Sully, and all of those caddies from Eddie's job, we're so grateful."

Frankie had a frown on his face, still reeling from the sting operation that Joe put on him, but he realized that Eddie didn't have much time, and he knew he needed to act fast. "Let's get something straight Mr. Mullaney. First of all, I'm not doing this for anyone other than Eddie. He's the only one I'm worried about right now."

"Okay," said Joe.

"Secondly, don't get too much of a hard-on just yet, because if you think I'm gonna tell you where Nino Grilli is, you're fuckin' insane. You see I'm not like you, I'm not a sneak and a liar. Before I tell you what I am about to tell you, I need to know that we're off the record."

"Absolutely, I'm listening," said Joe.

Frankie took a deep breath and let out a sigh. "We were open for business again the second you guys busted into the office. One of my guys was able to hit one of the speed-dial buttons that was set up on his phone. That button calls the beeper of a friend of mine, who will, of course, remain nameless. We're still off the record right?"

"Yes Frankie, I promise, go on."

"As soon as that beeper goes off, that person has one job. His job is to make sure that business continues. He stays off the phones. He gets in his car and drives around to our biggest customers, giving them a new number, so they can continue betting. He gets a crew over to my back-up office in Staten Island. We have a back-up office that looks exactly like the one you guys hit. Oh, and by the way, if you think that it's really in Staten Island, you're fuckin' dreamin'. Let's just say it's somewhere in the seven one eight area code."

"Go ahead," said Joe. Joe was actually laughing inside to himself. He could not believe that he was talking to a teenager. He hadn't laughed in weeks. He was listening attentively, and really getting a kick out of it as well. He was confused, but very interested as to how this could help Eddie.

Frankie continued again. "We were taking bets that same night. I just can't go near any of the money, obviously, and we lost a ton of guys after the bust. I have about twenty-six large that I want to give you towards Eddie's transplant costs. It's all I have left. I would have a lot more, but that one little over-zealous prick agent of yours, who was using my neck as a step stool, found a ton of loot in my wall. They also seized all of the cash I had stashed at the deli and at my house."

Joe smiled, and then interrupted, "But Frankie, I have medical coverage, that's not the problem. We just need a fucking donor. I don't know what the fuck to do Frankie, Eddie will die in less than two weeks!"

"Mr. Mullaney," said Frankie, as he was trying to speak above the uncontrollable lump that was developing in his throat. "You ever been to Mexico?"

Joe looked completely puzzled by the question. "No, never, why?"

"Well, guess what?" charged Frankie. "They do liver transplants in Mexico like they're puttin' on a fuckin' band-aid, and they don't ask you for your fuckin' insurance card when your plane lands either. It's all cash, and it's legal, too. Last year, they did between eight and ten successful transplants a week, in a small city called Guadalajara."

Joe looked intrigued. "How the hell do you know about all of this, Frankie?"

"You see, Mr. Mullaney, there is this doctor who bets with us every time there is a huge boxing match. His name is Dr. Sanchez. He lives right here in Brooklyn. He bets big, but he is so busy traveling back and forth to Mexico that he uses me, and the guys I work for, to take his bets instead of going to Vegas. I remember hearing about one of his operations a few months ago from one of his American patients who's a regular at the deli. The guy's name is Caden Reagan. His son plays Pop Warner football with Sanchez's kid. Dr. Sanchez was telling Caden that some rich dude flew his son to Mexico to get a transplant, and it fuckin' worked! The guy who got the transplant is alive and well and living in Boston. I've been tryin' to reach this doctor for a fuckin' week, hoping that he could give us some advice or something, fuckin' anything. He finally got back to me in the middle of the night."

Joe's eyeballs were popping out of his head. "What did he say?"

"He said that in Mexico there's no donor list or any of that bullshit. Bottom line, you got the cash, they'll give you a liver, period. The liver transplant working successfully, well that's a whole other story, but it's worth a shot."

Joe leaped out of his chair and began to pace around the living room, limping quickly in circles, and rubbing the top of his head. "That's it then," cried Joe. "Holy shit, that's it. What do we do now, and how much money will we need?"

"The guy who the doctor saved last year was out of pocket about four hundred grand," said Frankie.

"What?" screamed Joe.

"It's not just for the transplant, Mr. Mullaney. We'd have to charter a flight, hire a medical staff to travel with us, pay for all of the medical equipment, and set up ground transportation when we land."

Joe was now literally weeping, knowing full well that there was no way he could come up with that kind of money in that amount of time. He was in panic mode. "Frankie, between borrowing money on the house, and the money we raised last night, we're lucky if we have half that. There is no fuckin' way I can come up with that kind of money."

"Maybe not," said Frankie. "But I can."

Joe looked at Frankie, with dried-up tears on his cheeks and red circles around the rims of his eyes. "What are you talking about, Frankie?"

"You remember before when I said I wanted to cut a deal, Mr. Mullaney?"

"Yeah," said Joe.

"Well here's the fuckin' deal. There's this other guy who bets with us, just about every week. The guy is a fuckin' *whale*. He bets no less than ten thousand a game. He runs this fake stock company in the city. You know what this cocksucker does?"

"No," said Joe. "What?"

"He fuckin' cold calls people all over the country telling them about all of these stocks that don't even exist. He gets people who are great targets. People like my grandparents, people like your in-laws. He goes after anyone who doesn't know a thing about the stock market. The guy is a predator, Mr. Mullaney, and he makes millions of dollars robbing innocent people. If the Feds think bustin' me and Nino Grilli is a big score, wait until you get this guy. You'll get your fuckin' picture on the front page of the *New York Times* for this bust. You wanna hear more?"

Joe had no idea where Frankie was going with all of this but he played along. "What's the guy's name Frankie, and how can busting him help Eddie?"

Frankie continued. "His account number when he calls me to place a bet, is D-five four eight, and his password is 'Chief,' but his real name is Wally McDougal."

Joe turned ghost white, knowing that it had to have been the same guy he was picturing. He reached down with his left hand, clutching his prosthetic leg. The past seventeen years of his life had been spent in physical therapy, with a cane in his left hand, getting assistance when entering and exiting the car, sticking his fake leg out of the fuckin' shower, and having to position himself in certain ways when he was intimate with his wife. All of this was a result of this man, who never even had the decency to seek him out to thank him for saving his life.

The sound of the No. 2 subway train was ringing in his head, just like it did that day. He pictured himself leaping towards this guy and saving his life, leaving him with nothing but a severed limb, and years of rehab at the FBI treatment center. He was steaming mad, and now he was being told that there was a way to take this guy down, let his son's best friend go free, and help save his only son at the same time. He was all ears now, still squeezing his fake leg to the point that his fingertips were bright red with all of the blood that was rushing to them. His eyes were popping out of his head, and his mouth was wide open. Frankie had no idea that Joe knew this man, but he was happy that he was listening to his plan. Joe started to speak in a soft, silent, stunned tone, "I'm still listening Frankie."

"This son-of-a-bitch is a bad guy," said Frankie. "He makes so much money that he is able to have multiple offices all over the city so he has plenty of back-up space. He pays over three hundred grand a month for all of the places that he rents. He has a staff of about seventy people, and they are on the phones all day. They don't cold call wealthy guys, they go after strictly old people, or people who are just inexperienced investors."

"Continue," said Joe.

"These poor people think they're setting up their loved ones with a nice little portfolio, but instead, they just get fuckin' burnt on these bullshit stocks. How the fuck you guys don't know about this guy is a shock, I gotta be honest with you," said Frankie.

Joe moved up in his chair closer and closer to Frankie, with his eyes glued to Frankie's face.

Frankie continued. "McDougal's guys get so many people that it doesn't matter if they are only buying like twenty-five shares or something. He gets thousands upon thousands of people and he fuckin' wipes em' out, selling them phony business plans and company prospectuses. When he feels it's getting too hot, he and that whole crew of seventy pack up and move to the next office. They start up under a new name and start all over again. He's the king of the chop shops. Chop shops are actually more common than you think, from what I hear, but this guy is the biggest guy out there."

"Go on," said Joe.

Frankie continued. "This mutha fucka has been bettin' with Nino for over a year, and believe me, we love havin' a fuckin' guy like this around. The guy loses most of the time because he's a fuckin' drunken idiot. Not only that, but he also pays up immediately. It doesn't matter if he loses fuckin' twenty G's, he's always at the Thursday night meeting spot with a fuckin' bag full of money. That's fuckin' chump change to a guy like that anyway. Trust me, I've collected from him many times. I love when the scumbag loses, I get paid a quarter of it. Nino had a bad feeling about this guy the first time he looked into his eyes. Nino said he never could put his finger on it, but there was something about McDougal that just didn't sit right with him."

Joe interrupted Frankie. "Alright, so he bets a lot. So does half the world during football season, Frankie. I want to know how the hell you know about all of this other shit, and what the fuck does any of this have to do with helping my son?"

"Let me finish, Mr. Mullaney."

"Go on," said Joe, reluctantly.

"Although Nino never trusted McDougal, in our business, if a guy bets this much and pays up on time, you don't go cuttin' him off because you have a hunch about him. Nino's no fuckin' dummy. He had such a bad feeling about this guy that he's got a few guys working in McDougal's office right now. Nino sent them to interview with McDougal about three or four months ago and he hired them on the spot. The fuckin' guy hires anybody. Nino thought they'd be there for a couple of weeks, thinking there was no fuckin' way either one of them would pass the Series 7. Believe it or not, they both passed so Nino made them stay on for a while. Nino told them to gather as much shit on McDougal as they could, just in case he ever needed a little something to hold over on him."

"Holy shit," muttered Joe to himself. Joe moved a little closer to Frankie, staring straight at him. "What kind of information did they get?"

"Fuckin' everything!" cried Frankie. "They copied all of McDougal's shit onto floppy discs. Names of the scam victims, fake stock certificates, bullshit profit projections, phony corporate seals, offshore bank statements, totally fabricated business plans. Nino knows more about McDougal's fuckin' business than he does. Anyway, I got no problem rollin' over on a fuckin' asshole like McDougal. I feel he's worth takin' down and you're gonna help me do it, and I am gonna help you save Eddie."

Joe was growing impatient. "Okay but how, goddamn it?"

Frankie reached into his left pocket and pulled out five floppy discs that were rubber-banded together. He placed them on the oak coffee table in front of him. He still had not taken his eyes off of Joe. "McDougal called the new office yesterday, Mr. Mullaney. He wants to bet two hundred grand on the Super Bowl next week and he was just making sure we could take the bet. Under normal circumstances, we would never ever take a bet like that. We would lay it off to a guy from the Bronx who's a lot fuckin' bigger than we are. That guy will also remain nameless."

"Okay, I'm listening," said Joe.

Frankie's voice was rising more and more. "This time, I'm takin' the fuckin' action, and you're gonna let me!"

Joe was still paying very close attention but was not quite piecing everything together. "Okay, keep going, keep going!"

"As far as the Feds are concerned, the reason for my plea is just to hand you a fuckin' multi-million dollar scumbag who robs innocent people. They don't need to know a fuckin' thing about the bet. We just need to pray like hell that he loses, if not I'll have to fuckin' rob him or something."

Joe snickered.

"Relax," said Frankie. "I'm kidding. If he does happen to win, I'll have someone leak it to him that we got pinched by the cops, and we won't be able to pay him for about a week or two. We have a fuckin' week, Mr. Mullaney. When you see the shit that's on these discs you'll have enough fuckin' probable cause to get warrants or whatever other shit you guys need to put the prick away. All I need for you to do is to wait until the Super Bowl ends before turning these discs into evidence, without uttering the word 'plea' until next week, and pray your fuckin' ass off that McDougal does not win this bet."

Joe was looking Frankie right in the face with his eyes wide open. He could not believe that he was even entertaining any of this, but Frankie knew he was thinking about it. A full minute had passed and Joe hadn't said a fuckin' word yet. Frankie was sitting on the couch in the living room, and Joe was sitting back in his chair. Joe Mullaney was a good man, an ex-cop, a devoted husband and father, and a well-respected and admired Federal agent. He was as straight as they come. He was a man who used to make the eighth grade basketball team dress in shirts and ties when they were traveling to and from a game, making sure that each kid tied his own tie and wore it all the way up to his neck. Breaking rules was not something that he did. He knew that if he was going to take part in orchestrating such a plan, that he would be in serious fuckin' trouble if he ever got caught. He also knew that McDougal was a fuckin' scumbag, and if the information on these discs was accurate, the Feds would want to bring a guy like McDougal down. This moral dilemma had the righteous Joe Mullaney deep in thought as he pondered over each option in his head, ultimately knowing which choice he needed to make. He was rubbing his palms feverishly on his eyeballs and rocking back and forth in his chair. Frankie just kept staring at him. Joe was thinking ahead to what it would be like to watch his boy playing at Madison Square Garden as a college ball player, with his family and friends rooting him on as they were sitting courtside. He was smiling as he pictured Eddie coming off the bench against Syracuse on a cold Saturday afternoon the following year, with the crowd going wild for the local kid from Brooklyn, as he hit his first official shot as a Big East ball player. Suddenly, the image of Eddie in that hospital bed with fuckin' tubes running all through his body and his stomach enlarged was interrupting his beautiful thought, and bringing tears down his cheeks. He was sweating, rubbing his hands together at the very thought of losing his boy. He was staring straight down at the floor. Frankie started to move closer to him. Joe picked up his head, and looked right at Frankie, already knowing the answer to the question he was about to ask.

"And if he loses?"

Frankie got up from the couch and started to pace back and forth and run his fingers through his hair. He was speaking faster and louder. "If he loses the bet, you let me collect the money the very next day. Between the cash that I have outside in the car, the benefit money, McDougal's money, and the money from your house, Eddie will get a new liver, and he'll be fuckin' loopin' and hoopin' by the summer. Nino is so fuckin' happy that I've left his name out of all of this shit, he's letting me take this bet on my own to try to help my best friend. He doesn't want a fuckin' dime if this prick loses. Not such a bad guy after all, huh?"

Joe was stoic. He said nothing, but he loved the idea, and Frankie could tell. Frankie looked Joe square in his Irish mug. "We got a deal, Mr. Mullaney?"

Frankie didn't even need for Joe to open his mouth again, he already had his answer.

THE GREEN BAY PACKERS WERE heavily favored in Super Bowl XXXII, on January 25, 1998. Everyone was betting the Packers. Brett Favre was "the shit." Most gamblers figured that Green Bay was at least two touchdowns better than the Denver Broncos, but Frankie had no idea who McDougal was gonna bet.

Deep down, Frankie thought the same as the rest of the betting world and he prayed all fuckin' night that when McDougal called to place the bet, that he was gonna bet Denver. McDougal had a history of betting the underdog too, and nine times out of ten, if the line was in double digits, he took the points. McDougal never bet this much on a game. Frankie figured that he probably had a really good month of ripping people off, which made him root twice as hard that the scumbag loses the bet. He couldn't get Eddie out of his head. This plan had to work and he knew that.

The Green Bay Packers were favored by eleven and a half and Frankie was miserable when McDougal called and bet Green Bay, figuring Denver had no chance, even with the points. Frankie watched the game in his bedroom all by himself.

Joe was sitting in the lobby at the hospital, alone, having already gotten the call from Frankie, and ready to root for Denver like he was a fuckin' Colorado resident. Everything was set. There was no way Joe and Kathy were gonna just let their boy die, no fuckin' way, not without a fight and a prayer. They were able to reserve a private jet at Teterboro Airport, in New Jersey.

Dr. Lally had helped them hire a full nursing staff to accompany them on the plane. The Mullaney's were fully prepared to pay them in cash. If McDougal lost the bet, the plan was to collect the money on Monday afternoon and head to Mexico right away. With a bet that size, Frankie made sure to get McDougal on a taped line, saying that he had the money, in cash, and would be prepared to pay by the next day if he lost. Nino had a few of his guys in place keeping a close eye on McDougal, just in case he lost and decided to disappear. Frankie had everything set up with Dr. Sanchez and his staff at the hospital in Mexico. All they needed now was a miracle from the Denver Broncos.

Play-by-play announcer, Dick Enberg, and color commentators Phil Simms and Paul Maguire, were hosting the game that day, and they couldn't stop talking about the massive migraine headache that Denver's Terrell Davis had been suffering from, causing him to miss most of the second quarter. It was making Frankie sick.

Frankie had a computer mouse pad in his hand. He was

sitting on the end of his bed, screaming at the TV and slapping the mouse pad on his knee, praying that Denver's quarterback, John Elway, gets the first down as he was scrambling for an eight-yard run late in the third quarter.

Joe was making so much noise, he was holding Nino's stack of discs in his hand for good luck, crying and cheering at the same time, gripping the sweaty discs in his right hand and slapping them into his left on each play. People were walking through the lobby and staring at him in the corner, hopping up and down on his good leg. Eddie was in his room, asleep, with tubes running all through his body. Joe knew Eddie would be so happy if he knew what Frankie was doing for him. Joe continued screaming "Go Elway, go Elway, go Elway.......Yes!" Joe was going crazy.

John Elway converted the unlikely first down. He was hit so hard that his body looked like a helicopter before he landed back down on the field. Two plays later, Denver's Terrell Davis scored on a one-yard touchdown run to put the Broncos up 24-17, and McDougal down eighteen and a half to nothing.

The Broncos went on to win the game 31-24, without even needing the eleven and a half points. Frankie's plan fuckin' worked and he made sure he called McDougal right away to set up a meeting time for Monday afternoon.

Frankie collected the money from McDougal the next day. He borrowed Nicky Ventimiglia's car and was driving towards the hospital at about eighty miles per hour. He just had to tell Eddie that everything was going to be okay. Frankie was screaming all the way down the hallway of New York-Presbyterian. Doctors, nurses, and other visitors were stepping back, astounded by the amount of noise Frankie was making. Frankie was screaming, "Eddie we did it, Eddie boy, we fuckin' did it!" When he barreled through the door of Eddie's room, he screamed and cried, falling to his knees. Colleen, Kathy, and Joe, were all sitting on Eddie's bed. They were all saying their good-byes, but he was already gone.

Frankie was kneeling there, looking up in total disbelief, as Kathy was shutting Eddie's eyelids and placing her hand on his cheek. Frankie crawled on his knees over to the bed and grabbed Eddie's arm with one hand, and Colleen's arm with the other. They cried together, through the night.

ST. ELIZABETH'S CLOSED THE SCHOOL on the day of Eddie's funeral. St. Francis Church was packed with people for the 10:30 Requiem Mass. Frankie, Sully, Brian Quinn, and a few of the guys from the basketball team were the pallbearers. Every St. Elizabeth's junior and senior was there, along with hundreds of people from St. Francis parish. There wasn't a dry eye in the church, as Joe gave the eulogy for his boy. Eddie was everyone's favorite, and this loss was felt by everyone in the school, and in the neighborhood. Members of the Police Department's Emerald Society Pipe and Drum Corps lined the church steps and played "Amazing Grace" on the bagpipes as Eddie was being led out of the church. The funeral cortege was led by the NYPD with their lights flashing.

At the cemetery, while Eddie's friends and family walked back to their cars after saying their final goodbyes, Frankie stayed behind and knelt down by the green canvas covered dirt mound next to Eddie's coffin. He was crying his eyes out. "You son-of-a-bitch, I'm gonna miss you so much, bro. We made some team man, huh? Sorry I couldn't get you that state championship, man. I'm sorry that I lost my head that night."

Frankie was trying to finish saying goodbye to his friend, but he was having a tough time getting the words out. Frankie was always the tough guy, the chance-taker, and now he felt somewhat guilty that the kid who kept him in line just by being there for him, was gone. The skies were clear and there was old snow surrounding the gravesite.

"I just wanted you to know that you never took those Jordans for saving my ass at camp that day. I'll bring a pair up when it's my turn to go, okay? Can I ask you a favor, bro? When you find my dad, can you thank him for helping me catch McGlynn? I promise you, Eddie, I will take good care of Colleen, buddy, you have my word. I love you, man."

Frankie got up off the ground and wiped the mud off of his pants and the palms of his hands. He reached into his pocket and pulled out his Yankee World Series ticket stub. He tossed the stub on top of the flower-covered casket, pointed his left fist in the direction of the coffin to give his pal one final fist pound, and uttered his final words to Eddie. "I'll never forget that game, pal. Thank you for bringing me. Until we meet again, Eddie boy."

BROOKLYN LOOPER WON HER FIRST race up in Saratoga Springs, New York, on August 13, 2005. She was a beautiful three-year-old filly, purchased at a private sale in Ocala, Florida. The owners of the horse mobbed the winner's circle picture with their families and friends. They were so excited as they headed to Siro's, the most famous restaurant in Saratoga, to start their celebration.

Quinn-Morelli Asset Management was the name of the Wall Street hedge fund that sponsored the purchase of the horse. At the racetrack, the group went under the name *State Champ Stables*. The jockey wore the silks that were the exact color of the St. Elizabeth's home uniform, kelly-green and white.

The horse had originally been priced at $210,000. Frankie insisted on paying exactly $220,000, the exact amount that he collected from McDougal, seven years earlier. He didn't want any of that guy's money and was happy to pay a little extra for Eddie's horse.

Frankie smiled when he was reading the *New York Post* on the morning of the race. There was an article about Yankee great, Mickey Mantle. It was the tenth anniversary of his death, and the horse just happened to draw number seven. Frankie was certain that his dad had pulled that string for sure, and he knew this was gonna be Eddie's day.

I had four horses up for sale at the annual two-year-old auction in Maryland in 2004. *Brooklyn Looper,* originally named *Gratiaen Sensation,* in memory of the first horse that I bought about fifteen years ago with a bunch of my Little League buddies, was the only horse that was not purchased at the sale. I'm a big believer in fate. Maybe I had her priced too high for a reason. I hate assholes that talk about themselves in the third person, but I thought it was the best way to tell you the story of these two kids until the coast was clear. I miss the New York action, believe me, but the short time I got to spend with Frankie Morelli taught me what friendship and loyalty are all about. It also taught me that going with my gut was the right decision, and that when half of my crew told me that I was fuckin' nuts to let a kid that young take on such huge responsibilities, that they were dead wrong. My instincts were dead on.

When Frankie called me and said he was looking to buy a horse from me, I was surprised, at first, but I knew what he was lookin' to do. I always knew that this horse was gonna be special, and I thought that the new name that Frankie chose for her was fuckin' perfect.

I tried to refuse the extra ten grand for the horse, at first, but Frankie wanted me to have it. Frankie was always a man of his word and he was determined to make good on my little favor from the Super Bowl in '98. Even though Eddie's pop was tryin' to put me in jail, I always felt kinda bad for the guy after he lost his kid. I told Frankie that maybe he could use the money to do something nice for Eddie's family. After all, Agent Mullaney did show some pretty big balls to go along with our plan.

The relationship that I have with Frankie goes beyond the bullshit that you see in the movies or on television. I always knew that Frankie's brain would be better served working in a legit situation in finance, and I wasn't a bit surprised that he had made it. Frankie and I still remain close friends, and even meet for dinner once a year when I go up to New York for the Belmont Stakes, at a place called Fiore, Frankie's favorite Italian restaurant, near Belmont Racetrack in Floral Park. We finish off the evening right next door with a nightcap at J. Fallon's Tap Room, where the *Brooklyn Looper* winner's circle picture still hangs today.

The Feds never got me on a fuckin' thing, thanks to Frankie Morelli. From what I hear, I'm still on their watch list, but I'm old news. I look a bit different now anyway. It's amazing what a little plastic surgery and a diet of nothin' but bread and pasta can do for someone.

Eddie Mullaney was too young to have a will, but he did manage to do two things on the morning that he passed away. He was extremely weak, but he found enough energy to call Brian Quinn and ask him to give Frankie his internship. The second thing he did was to tell his sister to make sure that Frankie took the job with Brian, and never ever take another bet for the rest of his life. He told her that his buddy Frankie was twice as smart as he was, and that if he could do that well as a teenaged bookie, that he'd own Wall Street as an adult.

Frankie and Brian's firm currently manages 1.5 billion dollars, and has averaged a seventeen percent return for their investors since launching in 2003.

Eddie may have been gone, but he was at the track in spirit that day for sure. *Brooklyn Looper* won the race by six lengths, and paid $31.60. Frankie called a bunch of people that day, telling them there was no fuckin' way that this horse was losing. He called me, his uncles, the Goodfellas, and every single one of his and Eddie's teammates, a little monetary apology from Frankie to the team for his outburst that night in Albany. They all made a bundle.

Wally McDougal is doing twelve to fifteen in a Federal Detention Center in Oakdale, Louisiana. He was convicted on over a hundred counts of fraud, twenty-seven counts of forgery, thirteen counts of insider trading and grand larceny. Evidence found that Wally McDougal had stolen more than 23 million dollars from his pool of inexperienced investors, nationwide. With the exception of my two guys, who ironically quit two days before that Super Bowl, every one of McDougal's employees testified as to what their orders were under him. He will be eligible for parole in 2009.

Fuzzy McGlynn is serving four consecutive life sentences in an upstate penitentiary for the murder of Frankie's father, and three others.

Frankie and Colleen Morelli live in a huge two-story house, right on the beach, in Breezy Point, New York. Their son, Francis Edward Morelli, now fourteen months old, will grow up to be a Met fan, and that's fine with his dad.

The Edward J. Mullaney Memorial Caddy Golf Tournament is held on the first Monday in July at The Garden Oaks Country Club. The tournament is run by the Morelli and Mullaney families, and caddies must be entering their senior year in high school in order to participate. The winner receives a check for $25,000 towards the tuition of the college of his choice, donated by *State Champ Stables*.

Frankie brings breakfast and lunch for all of the caddies in the yard on that day. He then throws a couple of bags on his shoulders, and makes his one loop per year, free of charge of course, caddying for the two kids who advance to the final round, just as Eddie would have done.

The End